THE DEVIL IN LOVE

Barbara Cartland

Barbara Cartland Ebooks Ltd

This edition © 2023

Copyright Cartland Promotions 1975

ISBNs

9781788677127   EPUB

9781788677028   PAPERBACK

Book design by M-Y Books
m-ybooks.co.uk

THE BARBARA CARTLAND ETERNAL COLLECTION

The Barbara Cartland Eternal Collection is the unique opportunity to collect all five hundred of the timeless beautiful romantic novels written by the world's most celebrated and enduring romantic author.

Named the Eternal Collection because Barbara's inspiring stories of pure love, just the same as love itself, the books will be published on the internet at the rate of four titles per month until all five hundred are available.

The Eternal Collection, classic pure romance available worldwide for all time .

THE LATE DAME BARBARA CARTLAND

Barbara Cartland, who sadly died in May 2000 at the grand age of ninety eight, remains one of the world's most famous romantic novelists. With worldwide sales of over one billion, her outstanding 723 books have been translated into thirty six different languages, to be enjoyed by readers of romance globally.

Writing her first book 'Jigsaw' at the age of 21, Barbara became an immediate bestseller. Building upon this initial success, she wrote continuously throughout her life, producing bestsellers for an astonishing 76 years. In addition to Barbara Cartland's legion of fans in the UK and across Europe, her books have always been immensely popular in the USA. In 1976 she achieved the unprecedented feat of having books at numbers 1 & 2 in the prestigious B. Dalton Bookseller bestsellers list.

Although she is often referred to as the 'Queen of Romance', Barbara Cartland also wrote several historical biographies, six autobiographies and numerous theatrical plays as well as books on life, love, health and cookery. Becoming one of Britain's most popular media personalities and dressed in her trademark pink, Barbara spoke on radio and television about social and political issues, as well as making many public appearances.

In 1991 she became a Dame of the Order of the British Empire for her contribution to literature and her work for humanitarian and charitable causes.

Known for her glamour, style, and vitality Barbara Cartland became a legend in her own lifetime. Best remembered for her wonderful romantic novels and loved by millions of readers worldwide, her books remain treasured for their heroic heroes, plucky heroines and traditional values. But above all, it was Barbara Cartland's overriding belief in the positive power of love to help, heal and improve the quality of life for everyone that made her truly unique.

AUTHOR'S NOTE

It is greatly accepted that champagne was the result of Dom Perignon's life work. He was certainly the first man to produce sparkling champagne in France. But as Patrick Forbes shows in his brilliant history of *'Champagne'* it is equally certain that the English were quietly making champagne nearly a decade earlier.

There is no mention of champagne in French literature until around 1700, but in Butlin's *Hudibras*, first performed in 1666, it refers to champagne being 'brisk'.

"Drink every little l'it in stum (still wine)
And made it brisk Champaign become."

In Sir George Etherege's *'The Man and the Mode'* which opened in 1676, there were the lines,

"Then sparkling Champaign

Puts an end to their reign

It quickly recovers Poor languishing lovers".

As Patrick Forbes remarks, this 17th Century English champagne must have been primitive in the extreme. But the fact remains that the basic principle of manufacturing sparkling champagne, which Dom Perignon worked out for himself at Hautvillas, had already been discovered and drunk by the English.

CHAPTER ONE

"It has come! *It has come!*"

Larisa burst into the schoolroom with a letter in her hand and every face in the room was turned towards her.

A spectator when he looked at the Stanton family might have been excused for thinking that he had stumbled inadvertently onto an Olympian party dedicated to Venus.

Lady Stanton, who had been surpassingly beautiful in her youth, was now a little faded but her four daughters looked exactly like Greek goddesses.

The late Sir Beaugrave Stanton attributed their beauty to the fact that he himself was obsessed with ancient Greece and it had been his interest and occupation all his life. But their fair hair undoubtedly owed much to Lady Stanton's Scandinavian ancestors, although their classical features and perfectly proportioned bodies might have been inherited from their father.

It was due to their father's preoccupation that all the Stanton girls were Christened with Greek names.

Larisa was named after the town where he had stayed on his first visit to the country while Cynthus, Athene and Delos were all baptised with names he found in his research, in which he was absorbed at the time of their arrival.

Sir Beaugrave's only son, who had now inherited the baronetcy, had been called Nicias, a name that embarrassed him and so, during his school days, had been modified to the more mundane 'Nicky'.

Nicky seemed as interested as his sisters in the letter that Larisa held in her hand and which she gave to her mother.

"Here it is, Mama."

Her blue eyes held a hint of anxiety as her mother took the letter from her and without hurrying opened the envelope.

There came a hush over the family assembled in the schoolroom as if they all waited breathlessly to know what Larisa's fate was to be – and incidentally Nicky's.

It had been Larisa, who although not the oldest of the four sisters, was the most practical, and who had lifted them from a helpless depression when after Sir Beaugrave's death they realised the impecunious state in which they had been left.

While their father had been alive he had dealt with the financial affairs of the family.

Although he continually preached prudence and economy, it had not seemed imperative until they learnt when he died exactly how precarious their situation was.

"Did you realise, Mama," Nicky had asked incredulously, "that Papa had spent all his capital?"

"I always left such things to him," Lady Stanton had murmured apologetically.

"But you knew how hopeless he was about such matters," Nicky said accusingly. "After all he lived in a world of his own and the only coinage with which he was concerned was that used by the ancient Greeks!"

"Yes, I know, *I know,*" Lady Stanton replied unhappily, "but it bored your father to talk of money – and somehow we always managed to have enough to eat and to pay the servants' wages."

"Only because every year he was dipping into his capital," Nicky said sharply, "and now there is nothing left, Mama. Do you understand? *Nothing!*"

For a little while the family was too stunned to understand what this could mean. They had lived in the comparatively large Redmarley House in Gloucestershire all their lives and it had been the Stantons' family seat for three centuries.

Their great-grandfather, the fifth Baronet, had in the middle of the 18th Century altered the house considerably, adding to it a Georgian portico with impressive Ionic columns, which had always delighted their father.

It stood high on a hill with the parkland sloping away into the valley and there was only a small hamlet with a dozen cottages surrounding a Norman church in the immediate vicinity.

The Stanton daughters did not feel isolated.

They had their horses to ride and they were so happy with each other that they did not miss the companionship of their neighbours and friends – all of whom lived so far away that the family's only visitors were limited to perhaps a dozen a year.

It was Nicky as he grew up who complained of lack of entertainment and who in consequence found Oxford alluring and delightful, as did most young men of his age.

Nevertheless, he worked hard because ever since he was a small boy it had been agreed that he should go into the Diplomatic Service. It was on his father's death that he was forced to face the fact that as things were, it would be almost impossible for him to continue at Oxford, and he would therefore not get a First Class degree, which was essential in his chosen profession.

"What else can you do if you do not become a diplomat?" Larisa asked.

"I suppose I can always be a farm labourer if we can afford to keep the land!" he replied bitterly.

"I doubt if anyone would buy it in this isolated part of the country," Lady Stanton answered. "And besides, the Stantons have always lived here."

"Then I shall be the first Baronet not to do so," Nicky retorted.

It was Larisa who said firmly,

"We have to do something – all of us – to keep Nicky at Oxford until he receives his degree."

Her mother stared at her incredulously.

"What can we do?" Athene asked.

She was seventeen and a year younger than Larisa.

"That is what we have to decide," Larisa replied.

It had taken days and a great deal of argument before finally a plan was approved by them all.

When the controversy became too violent, Larisa always brought them back with the practical statement,

"We have to pay Nicky's fees."

It was finally decided that Lady Stanton, Athene and Delos, who was only fifteen, should move into a cottage on the estate. The big house would be shut up and what servants remained, with the exception of their old nurse, would be dismissed or pensioned off.

The land would be let to tenant farmers and although this would bring in a little money it was still not enough.

Cynthus, aged nineteen, was engaged to be married to the son of a local Squire.

He had only a small allowance from his father and they all decided it would be impossible to expect either him or Cynthus to contribute towards Nicky's education. At the same time Cynthus would play her part by not having any dowry on her marriage and costing nothing for her keep after she had left them.

While the discussions were still going on, Athene surprised them all by going out on her own one morning and returning with the news that she had found herself a job.

"I do not believe it!" Cynthus cried and Lady Stanton asked nervously, "what is it, Athene?"

"Do you remember old Mrs. Braybrooke?" Athene asked, "who lives at The Towers?"

"Yes, of course," Lady Stanton replied. "Although your father would not allow me to call on her – as her family is in commerce – I have occasionally bowed to her when leaving Church."

"Well, she is rich!" Athene said, "and I heard, because the butcher told Nurse when he called, that she was looking for someone to write her letters and be a kind of companion-secretary."

No-one spoke as Athene continued,

"I called on her and suggested that I could assist her and she is delighted at the idea!"

"How could you do such a thing without consulting me?" Lady Stanton asked.

"I had the feeling you would say no," Athene answered. "You know how stuffy Papa was about her – just because her husband made carpets in Kidderminster!"

"Is that what he did?" Nicky asked with interest.

"Actually, she is rather a nice old thing," Athene said, "and I am sorry for her because her family seldom comes to see her and she is very lonely now that she is a widow."

"What is her house like?" Delos asked irrepressibly.

"Very rich and grand," Athene answered. "The carpets are so thick your feet sink into them. The curtains look very new and are absolutely bristling with tassels and there is a whole army of servants falling over each other!"

"How much is she going to pay you?" Larisa asked.

"You will be astonished when I tell you," Athene said. "Hold your breath!"

They all waited until she said triumphantly,

"£100 a year! What do you think of that? And I need only be at The Towers for three or four hours a day unless she particularly wants me to stay longer."

"It is too much!" Lady Stanton said quickly. "You cannot accept it!"

"I *have* accepted it, Mama," Athene replied, "and you must realise that as I shall have no expenses, Nicky can have all of it, every penny!"

"I think it is very good of you, Athene," Nicky said, "and after all it does mean that you will still be living with Mama."

He looked at his mother as he spoke and Lady Stanton understood what he was trying to say to her.

Athene was the impetuous, impulsive member of the family, and Lady Stanton had already confided to her son that she was worried as to what might happen to her third daughter if she went away from home.

She was so lovely with her fair hair and her large blue eyes, which invariably held a hint of mischief, that any mother would have been afraid of what the future might hold.

In fact, Lady Stanton worried about all her daughters.

She had always hoped that they would be able to enjoy the gaieties and the social amusements that had been a part of her own girlhood.

But when Cynthus, the eldest, grew up she learnt, although she did not quite realise at the time how serious the situation was, that there was no money for frivolities.

It was true there always seemed to be enough money for the newest books about Greece and, twice after he had been married, Sir Beaugrave had gone abroad by himself to visit the land that haunted his dreams.

He had travelled, he assured his wife, in the very cheapest way, which was why he could not take her with him.

Nevertheless, the journeys made an increasing hole in his capital – and everyday expenses had finally swallowed it up entirely.

"How could Papa have gone on year after year spending and spending, without realising the day would come when there would be nothing left?" Nicky asked furiously.

"I am afraid your Papa never looked forwards," Lady Stanton answered. "He was always living in the past."

"That was all right for him," Nicky said bitterly, "but we have to go on living, and odes written to the Greek Islands are not going to pay the tradesmen's bills or my expenses at Oxford!"

It was understandable, the whole family thought, that Nicky should be the most incensed at their impoverished condition. He was the one who would suffer most.

What made it worse in some ways was that only at the end of last term his tutor had written a glowing account of his progress and how proud they had every reason to be of him.

With Cynthus engaged to be married and therefore no drain on their future expenditure, and Athene aged seventeen and earning money, Larisa waited apprehensively while her mother read the letter that had just arrived from London.

It was Larisa who had thought of writing to her Godmother Lady Luddington to ask if she could recommend for her a situation as a governess.

As Lady Stanton had sat down at her desk and started the letter in her elegant handwriting, she hoped almost against hope that her old friend would be generous enough to invite Larisa to London for a short visit.

But Larisa had entertained no such hopes.

She had met Lady Luddington once when she was fifteen and had realised far more clearly than her father and mother were apparently able to do that the worldly, elegant woman with her artificially preserved attractions was not likely to concern herself with the socially unimportant but very beautiful Stantons.

Larisa was the cleverest of Sir Beaugrave's daughters.

They were all highly intelligent and, having been given an intensive, if slightly unbalanced education by their father, were much better read and far more knowledgeable than the average young women of their age and social position.

Because Sir Beaugrave wished his daughters to help him, in what he called his research into Greek history, they could all speak Greek and write it with an elegance that also required precision.

Sir Beaugrave himself was bilingual in English and French – his grandmother had been a Frenchwoman.

When it suited him, he would speak French at meal times and nothing annoyed him more than not to be answered in the same language in vocabulary as extensive as his own.

History and Geography were of course part of the background of his beloved studies and therefore his children were obliged to become as proficient in them as he was himself.

Only in mathematics, which bored him, was there a gap in their knowledge that made Larisa say ruefully,

"I shall have to buy a book, Mama, on simple Arithmetic. I can hardly teach my pupils to count as I do on my fingers!"

"You will soon be able to mug it up," Athene remarked irrepressibly, only to be rebuked by her mother for using such a vulgar word. "Nicky uses it!" she protested.

"It may be suitable for Nicky, but it is certainly not suitable for you!" Lady Stanton pointed out. "We may be poor but we can still behave like cultured, civilised human beings."

"I only hope that the people we work for will recognise our worth!" Athene answered pertly.

Privately when she was alone with Larisa she said,

"I do not envy you being a governess. It is a horrid position. You are not grand enough for the drawing room and too grand for the servants' hall."

"What else am I capable of doing?" Larisa asked. "At least like Cynthus I shall be kept, so that every penny I earn I can give to Nicky."

This was indisputable.

At the same time, it was Larisa and not Athene who realised how many difficulties lay ahead of her.

First and foremost was the fact that she was so young.

Also, somewhere at the back of her practical little mind was the idea that ladies like her Godmother Lady Luddington would not be particularly anxious to employ someone so attractive that their own charms suffered in contrast.

Larisa would have been a fool, which she was not, if she did not realise that her whole family caused a sensation whenever they were seen by any member of the public.

Unfortunately, it did not work to their advantage.

Neighbours who had marriageable daughters took every care not to ask the Stanton girls to parties where their own offspring were expected to shine.

But now after ten days delay Lady Luddington had replied and, as she finished reading the letter, Lady Stanton put it down on her lap with a sigh.

"What does she say, Mama?" Athene asked eagerly before Larisa could speak. "Has she any good suggestions?"

"I do not know what to think," Lady Stanton murmured.

"Do let me hear what she has to say," Larisa begged.

Lady Stanton picked up the letter again.

"I will read it to you," she said and did so in the soft, musical voice that had always pleased her husband,

"'My dear Margaret, Your letter came as a great surprise as I must admit that I missed reading of the death of your husband in The Morning Post. I can only offer my somewhat belated condolences and my deepest sympathy. I know how fond you were of each other and how deeply you will miss him.

It is moreover with great regret that I hear he had left you in difficult circumstances and that my God-daughter Larisa is therefore obliged to find some sort of employment.

You ask me whether I know of a position as a governess in a well-connected family where she would be welcomed despite her extreme youth.

When I received your request, I searched among my many acquaintances for someone in need of such a teacher for their children. Unfortunately, at the moment, there is no-one in England as far as I know who would consider Larisa at the age of eighteen, preferring, not unnaturally, much older women with more stability and experience.

It happened by chance however that my dear and valued friend, the Comtesse de Chalon, was passing through London and came to dinner. During the course of the conversation, she informed me that her brother, the Comte de Valmont requires an English governess for his grandson to whom he is devoted.

This means of course that Larisa would have to go to France to live at Valmont-sur-Seine. I, naturally, having the interests of your family, dear Margaret, at heart enquired whether Larisa would be properly chaperoned, although it is not a question that would trouble one's head about an ordinary governess.

The Comtesse assured me that the Comte has his widowed sister, Madame Savigny, with him in the Château and that they live a very quiet life on their family estate.

This is what I am sure you would wish for Larisa, as the temptations and extravagances of Paris, which is now called the 'most debauched city in the world', would certainly not be suitable for a young girl.

Furthermore, I learnt from the Comtesse that the Comte de Valmont is well over sixty and, although a well-preserved man, has always been known for his austerity combined with a deep sense of responsibility towards those he employs.

I feel sure, my dear friend, that you can trust that Larisa will be safe in such an environment and on my recommendation the Comtesse has written to her brother to appraise him of Larisa's qualifications for tutoring his grandson.

I can only hope that Larisa will realise what a privilege this is for a young girl so inexperienced in the ways of the world and that she will behave, as might be expected of your daughter, in the best traditions of an English Lady.

I send you, dear Margaret, my thoughts and prayers during this sad and tragic time,

Yours affectionately,
Helen.'"

There was silence as Lady Stanton finished reading the letter and then Athene cried impulsively,

"*France!* You are going to France! Goodness, how lucky you are. I only wish it was me!"

"I am not certain I ought to accept such a suggestion," Lady Stanton said with a troubled look on her face.

"I cannot see why not, Mama," Cynthus exclaimed.

"It is so far away!" Lady Stanton murmured. "Besides, whatever Helen Luddington may say, Valmont-sur-Seine is very near Paris."

"Larisa certainly will not have any money to go gadding about in the wicked city!" Nicky interposed. "But I must say I envy her."

"As Mama said," Larisa said slowly speaking for the first time, "I shall doubtless lead a very quiet existence in the country, and I am no more likely to sample the excitements of Paris there than I am living here."

"I should hope not!" Lady Stanton said quickly. "From all I have heard it is very depraved."

"But very beautifully dressed!" Athene said irrepressibly. "All the best gowns in *The Ladies Journal* are Parisian models."

"And that certainly will not concern me as I shall not be able to afford even one of them!" Larisa smiled.

"You will need some new clothes all the same," Cynthus said. "You cannot go to France wearing the rags you are in now!"

Larisa looked down at her gown, which had once belonged to Cynthus, and had been passed on to her and would in its turn go on to Athene.

"It will soon be summer," she answered. "I can easily make myself some muslin gowns very cheaply. No-one will expect a governess to be smart."

They would certainly be suspicious if she were!" Nicky said.

"Suspicious of what?" Delos asked.

"That she was being – extravagant," Lady Stanton said quickly.

"How could she be extravagant if she did not have any money?" Delos enquired.

"We really need not concern ourselves with such ridiculous questions," Lady Stanton replied. "Larisa will have some gowns to go to France and we shall all have to help her make them."

"Surely it depends, Mama, upon whether I get the position," Larisa said. "We now have to wait until a letter arrives from the *Comte*."

"Yes, of course," Lady Stanton agreed, "perhaps there will not be one after all."

She seemed almost pleased at the idea.

But Larisa knew that if the *Comte* did not want her, the only alternative would be for her to write to one of the domestic bureaux that catered for out-of-work governesses.

She had the feeling there would not be many employers on their books willing to engage a governess of eighteen however distinguished her family background.

The governesses they had when they themselves had been small had all been women of about forty, clergymen's or doctor's daughters.

They had seemed resigned to their rather colourless lives and they had in fact lasted a very short time in the Stanton household simply because Sir Beaugrave found them so irritating.

"They know less than a child of ten!" he had stormed one, "and they never have a thought that is not written down in their lesson books!"

"What can you expect, dearest, for £50 a year?" Lady Stanton had asked.

"A human being for one thing!" Sir Beaugrave had snapped.

Governesses had come and gone until he had refused to employ any more of them and taught his daughters himself.

Nicky had of course gone to school and then to Oxford, and although Larisa sometimes envied her brother because his horizons were so much broader than theirs, she was on the whole very happy.

It hurt her now to think it was not only penury that faced them but the breaking up of the family.

She had known it was inevitable when Cynthus became engaged to be married, and she had thought that one day she too would fall in love and be loved in return.

Only when that happened had she envisaged herself going off on her own into the world outside of which she knew so little.

But while Larisa dreamt romantic dreams of the happiness she would one day find of loving and being loved, she was still the most practical of the Stanton girls.

She certainly had much more common sense than their sweet, feminine, helpless mother who had always depended for everything upon her husband.

"How shall I ever cope, Larisa," she asked despairingly, "in a tiny cottage without a cook or any other servants?"

"You will have Nana," Larisa answered, "and Delos enjoys cooking. Besides, Mama, you eat so little, there will not be so many big meals to prepare as when Papa was alive."

"I cannot imagine leaving here where I have lived since I was first married," Lady Stanton cried.

As she spoke, she looked around the drawing room with its high ceiling, fine Georgian cornice and long windows opening out to the terrace.

"I know, Mama," Larisa said sympathetically, "but you would

have had to leave it one day when Nicky married, and the Dower House – if we had not been lucky enough to let it – would have been too big for just you and two girls."

"I like big houses," Lady Stanton said petulantly, then added quickly, "but I must try to make the cottage look pretty. We can none of us bear anything ugly, can we?"

"No, of course not," Larisa answered. "It was Papa who taught us to appreciate beauty. Do you remember the rude things he used to say about antimacassars and too many tassels and frills?"

Lady Stanton laughed although there had been tears in her eyes.

It was true that Sir Beaugrave had given them all an appreciation of the exquisite lines of Greek antiquity. He disliked and disparaged all the clutter and furbelows so beloved of Queen Victoria.

Redmarley House with its Georgian simplicity and furnishings, which had been put there by his grandfather at the end of the 18th century, seemed sparse and empty compared with the houses of their friends.

But the girls knew that it was in impeccable and ageless good taste.

The beaded cushions, the dusty aspidistras, the doilies and the hair-tidies of their contemporaries were all fads of fashion that were only enjoyed by those who were ignorant.

The letter from the Comte de Valmont arrived four days later.

During the intervening time, Lady Stanton had been beset by so many doubts and so much anxiety that Larisa had begun to think that it would be impossible even if she were offered it, to accept a situation that would so greatly perturb her mother.

The *Comte's* letter was however in some ways reassuring.

Brief and formal, he merely said he had heard from his sister the Comtesse de Chalon that the services of Miss Larisa Stanton were available as a teacher of English and other elementary lessons for his grandson, Jean-Pierre de Valmont, aged eight.

He would therefore be pleased if Miss Stanton would proceed to France as soon as possible.

He was prepared to offer her a salary of three thousand, seven hundred and fifty francs per year and he enclosed her Second Class ticket from London to Paris, which included accommodation on the channel steamer.

If Lady Stanton, the *Comte* went on, would kindly let him know on which day her daughter would be arriving, he would arrange for her to be met at the *Gare du Nord* in Paris.

From there she would be conveyed by carriage to the Château Valmont where he would be waiting to instruct her in her duties.

It was a cold, business-like letter, which somehow pleased Lady Stanton far more than anything effusive or flowery could have done.

"Second Class!" Athene exclaimed. "Well that shows you right away, Larisa, what your place is now that you are a governess!"

"I naturally did not expect the *Comte* to pay for me to travel First Class," Larisa replied.

"Papa always said," Athene retorted, "that gentlemen travel First Class, businessmen Second and the peasants Third. You are in with the businessmen, Larisa!"

"Larisa will find a carriage marked 'Ladies Only'," Lady Stanton said. "I am sure they have them in France as they do in this country, and there will be no question of her speaking to businessmen or to any other type of man!"

She gave a deep sigh.

"Oh, Larisa, it is such a long way for you to go alone!"

"I can look after myself, Mama," Larisa answered.

The letter arrived when they had all assembled for lunch. Suddenly Nicky gave a shout.

"Good Heavens!" he exclaimed.

"What is it?" Larisa asked apprehensively.

"Do you realise how much the *Comte* is paying you?" he asked. "£150 a year!"

The others gave an audible gasp of astonishment.

"Are you sure?" Lady Stanton asked. "I am afraid I have no idea what the exchange is at the moment."

"It is about twenty-five francs to the pound," Nicky answered.

"Can he really mean me to have as much as that?" Larisa enquired.

"He has put it in writing," Nicky said.

"Then it is too marvellous!" Lady Stanton exclaimed. "With Athene's money and Larisa's you will have £250 a year! That should enable you to stay at Oxford until you have passed your examinations."

"It will indeed," Nicky said. "But Larisa must keep something for herself. She cannot be completely penniless in a strange land."

"No, you are right," Lady Stanton agreed, "but she will not need much."

"I shall need very, very little," Larisa interposed. "After all they will feed and keep me, and anything else I want I shall just have to go without!"

If you go to Paris you can always window-shop," Athene suggested.

Lady Stanton gave a little start as if she had forgotten Paris.

"You will have to promise me Larisa," she said, "that you will never go to Paris alone."

"I am quite sure no-one will expect her to do so, Mama," Cynthus said. "You know quite well that none of us would walk about alone in London, so why should Larisa do so in Paris?"

"No, of course not," Lady Stanton agreed, "and anyway I am sure there would be a maid who would go with you if by any chance you have to buy something for the little boy."

"You are not to worry, Mama," Larisa said soothingly. "Just think of it as an adventure. I promise that if it is not suitable I will come home."

She smiled.

"I am sure you will find room for me in the cottage. Nana has already decided that you are going to keep hens, so at least I shall be able to eat eggs, if there is nothing else!"

Nicky got up from the table.

"Now listen, all of you," he said, "I am deeply grateful for all you are doing for me but let us get one thing clear. Mama and the girls must have enough for food, clothes and wages."

He paused.

"I have arranged that the money from the rents from the farms will be entirely for their use. What Larisa and Athene are kind enough to give me and the few things we can sell out of the house will give me more than enough for my needs."

"Sell? What are you going to sell?" Lady Stanton cried.

"None of the furniture or pictures," Nicky assured her.

"They are, as you know, heirlooms and have been passed down from father to son, but I think some of Papa's books are first editions and the silver that was bought by grandpapa is not really important for future generations."

Lady Stanton sighed.

"I hate to think of us selling anything."

"It is better that, than any of us going hungry," Nicky replied, "and Larisa has to have some new gowns. I am not having my sister go to France looking like a beggar!"

"No, of course not," Lady Stanton agreed.

"As soon as I get my degree," Nicky said, "I shall be earning enough to spare something for all of you."

His mother looked at him with adoring eyes and only Larisa knew that while it sounded extremely gallant, Nicky would find it very hard indeed to live on his salary for the first years after he became a diplomat. She was quite sure that most young men in the same position had private incomes, but there was no use in crossing this particular bridge until they came to it.

In the meantime, thanks to Athene and herself and the few things they could sell, he would be able to finish his education at Oxford.

She was not as shocked as the rest of the family at the idea of selling their possessions.

She had already discussed it with Nicky and had helped him to sort out the books that she was sure would bring in some money, if not all that their father paid for them.

Many of them had been expensive.

There were also some archaic urns and other pieces of pottery that Sir Beaugrave had brought back from Greece on his visits and which they were both sure would be bought by a museum.

Things, indeed, were not quite so black as they had appeared at first when their father had died.

At the same time, it was going to be a wrench to leave the house, and they were both well aware how much Lady Stanton would hate the cramped little cottage where there would be little for her to do.

That evening when Larisa and Nicky were in the library looking at the books that were to go to London she had an idea.

"I think what Mama minds, although she has not said so, is the fact that we are all doing something for you except her."

She paused and added with a smile,

"You know she loves you more than all of us put together!"

"That is not true," Nicky protested rather half-heartedly.

"Of course it is true – and you know it!" Larisa said. "Mothers always love their sons best just as Papa preferred his daughters."

"His four Venuses," Nicky said with a smile. "He never could decide which of you was the most beautiful."

"I always used to think he preferred Cynthus," Larisa said, "but she thought he preferred Athene until Delos was born."

"You are all jolly good-looking," Nicky said, "and by the way, Larisa, look after yourself in France, you know that Frenchmen have a reputation where women are concerned."

"A reputation for what?" Larisa asked.

"Sweeping women off their feet!" Nicky replied. "Romeo and Juliet stuff! All that kissing the hand and looking at them with dark, eloquent eyes. You will have to keep your feet firmly on the ground or you will find yourself in trouble!"

"What sort of trouble?"

Nicky looked embarrassed.

"If you ask me, I think Mama ought to have a talk with you before you go," he said.

"I cannot think what you are fussing about," Larisa answered.

When she went to bed that night she found herself thinking of what Nicky had said. 'How do Frenchmen make love?' she wondered.

Sometimes she had thought how wonderful it would be to fall in love and know a man loved her in return.

'I love you!'. She could almost hear a man's deep voice say the words. He would put his arms round her and draw her close and then his lips would seek hers.

What would she feel? Would it be frightening? What was a kiss like?

She could find no answers to her questions.

Nevertheless, it was obvious that Nicky had spoken to his mother because a day or so later Lady Stanton called Larisa into her bedroom.

"I want to talk to you, Larisa…" she began.

"I want to talk to *you*, Mama," she answered. "I have had the most stupendous idea! I thought about it the other day when I was with Nicky in the library, but I did not want to say anything about it until I had discovered if it was practical."

"If what is practical?" Lady Stanton asked.

When I went into Gloucester yesterday," Larisa answered, "to buy the material for my gowns, I went with Nana to the toy shop in the High Street."

Lady Stanton looked bewildered.

"What did you go there for?"

I remembered the lovely dolls you used to buy there when we were children," Larisa said. "Some of them were dressed, but you always made them extra clothes. I remember what fun it used to be dressing and undressing my doll who was called Masera!"

She laughed.

"Of course, Papa chose her name! She did, not look a bit Greek but was very fashionable and elegant in her small crinoline and carrying the little sunshade, which you copied from one in *The Ladies Journal*."

"I remember how much I used to enjoy dressing your dolls," Lady Stanton said with a smile.

"Well, Mama," Larisa continued breathlessly, "you can make quite a lot of money dressing dolls for other children."

"What do you mean?" Lady Stanton asked.

"I inquired at the toy shop whether they had any demand for elegantly-dressed dolls and they told me that at Christmas time they could sell as many as they had in stock. I talked to the manager and he told me how we could buy the dolls very cheap. I think he called it wholesale. And when you have dressed one he will tell you how much he will give you for it."

"Larisa!" Lady Stanton exclaimed. "What would your father say?"

"I think even Papa would consider this legitimate trading," Larisa answered, "especially if the money goes towards Nicky's fees at Oxford."

"It certainly is an idea," Lady Stanton said slowly. "I do hope I can do it well enough."

"Of course you can, Mama," Larisa answered. "You know how badly most dolls are dressed. Yours would be exquisite! And you could do all sorts of different costumes, Spanish . . . Dutch . . . Eastern. It would be fun!"

"I will certainly try," Lady Stanton said, "and Nana could take them to the shop. I could not go myself. It would be really too embarrassing to sell, where I have always bought in the past."

"Oh no, of course not, Mama," Larisa said. "Athene can go with Nana. She is much sharper than the rest of us and I am sure she would not allow the manager to do you down."

"It sounds distressingly . . . commercial, Lady Stanton hesitated, "at the same time it is for Nicky."

"Do not think of anyone else, Mama," Larisa begged. "Just remember Nicky and I will tell Athene what to do."

Lady Stanton was silent for a moment and then she said,

"You have side-tracked me, Larisa. I wanted to talk to you about yourself."

"What did you want to say, Mama?"

"If you are going to France, dearest, I feel and so does Nicky, that I should give you a few words of advice before you set off on this rather frightening journey."

"I do not find it frightening, Mama . . . well not very!"

She paused a moment and then added,

"I suppose really I am frightened of doing the wrong things, of being sent home as being inadequate for the situation."

"It is not that of which I am frightened," Lady Stanton said.

"Then what is worrying you, Mama?"

Lady Stanton seemed to be choosing her words with care.

"You see, dearest," she began, "Frenchmen are different from Englishmen."

Larisa smiled.

"They speak a different language for one thing."

"This is not a joke," Lady Stanton admonished.

"I am sorry, Mama, go on."

"They have the reputation," Lady Stanton continued, "of being very dashing and irresistible to women."

"Are you warning me, Mama, against falling in love with a Frenchman?" Larisa asked.

"Yes, I am," Lady Stanton said, "and listen to me very carefully, Larisa, because it is important."

"I am listening."

Larisa was surprised at the note of seriousness in her mother's voice.

"You see, Larisa," Lady Stanton said, "an Englishman, if he is a gentleman, does not pursue a young girl unless his intentions are honourable, and he means to offer her marriage."

She sighed.

"At the same time, I understand governesses are in a class of their own. They are ladies and yet they are not considered eligible."

"Then what do you mean by 'pursue', Mama?" Larisa asked.

There was a long silence. Then Lady Stanton said,

"A man would try to make love to such a woman, Larisa."

"Like kissing her?"

"Yes"

"But the governess could always refuse."

"Which I am sure you would do," Lady Stanton said quickly. "Yet had you been going to an English household I would have warned you to be very circumspect and keep yourself apart from the gentlemen of the household."

She paused and added more brightly,

"Even so I cannot believe that the ordinary Englishman in the sort of house in which you will be employed would behave anything but decently towards a young woman who is unprotected and in a position where she is most vulnerable."

Larisa did not answer, but her eyes were on her mother's face as Lady Stanton went on,

"I will not disguise the fact from you, Larisa, that I hoped, perhaps rather foolishly, that if you did go into a house of one of your Godmother's friends you might meet someone who would fall in love with you and wish to marry you."

She gave one of her deep sighs.

"It is so isolated here. We see so few young men. But I would like above all things, my dearest, for you to have a happy marriage, as I had with your father."

Larisa wanted to say that this was what she too would like, but she knew her mother had more to say and did not wish to be interrupted.

"But in France it is very different," Lady Stanton went on.

"In what way?" Larisa enquired.

"French marriages are arranged, as I am sure you already know," Lady, Stanton said. "A Frenchman considers it his duty to take as his wife someone who has been chosen for him usually by his father because the girl will bring into the family land and a dowry. These of course vary according to the position he can offer her."

"You mean, Mama, that if a French girl married a Marquis her dowry must be higher than if she marries a *Comte*?" Larisa asked.

"Again, it depends on how important the family may be. It is not only the title. In France breeding and blood means more than anything else."

"What you are saying, Mama, is that if a Frenchman of good social standing did fall in love with me, he would not dream of asking me to become his wife."

"It is inconceivable that he should do so," Lady Stanton answered. "The head of the family is all-powerful. He holds all the money and doles it out as he thinks fit to his relations."

She smiled.

"That is why you will find in many cases a family house is packed not only with the father, mother and the children, but also with grandparents, aunts, uncles and cousins. It is so much cheaper to keep them all together under one roof than to give them enough money for separate establishments."

Larisa laughed.

"I always heard that the French are practical!"

"They are," Lady Stanton said, "so do remember that, Larisa! At the same time Frenchmen appreciate beautiful women and you are very lovely."

Larisa looked at her mother in surprise.

It was seldom Lady Stanton paid any of her daughters such a compliment.

"I am not making you conceited," she said, "because you are well aware already that your father thought you all looked like Greek goddesses."

"Four Venuses!" Larisa smiled. "And Nicky could be Apollo!"

"Yes, he could, could he not?" Lady Stanton replied with a softness in her voice. "I do not believe that any young man could be more handsome."

With an effort she brought her thoughts away from her beloved son back to her daughter.

"You must go to France, Larisa," she said, "with your pretty head screwed firmly onto your body. Do not listen if a Frenchman pays court to you. Do not believe a word he says about having fallen in love with you."

She spoke most impressively as she added,

"You have no dowry and although we can be proud of our ancestry, it will not count in France beside the fact that you are in the position of what is really a superior servant."

"I will keep my ears firmly closed, Mama, and I will not fall in love!" Larisa promised.

"Remember that to do so would be disastrous as far as you are concerned," Lady Stanton said. "It will only break your heart – and the man you love will marry someone else who can bring him money or land and who will gain the approval of his all-powerful family."

Larisa laughed.

"You make Frenchmen sound odious!" she said, "but I promise you, Mama, I will be on my guard against even the smallest compliment."

"I am speaking very seriously, Larisa."

"I know you are, Mama!"

She bent down to kiss her mother's cheek.

"Do not look so anxious," she begged. "I assure you that if none of your other children know how to look after themselves, I do!"

CHAPTER TWO

Larisa watched the white cliffs of Dover receding into the distance and then as the wind was strong went below.

There was a seat reserved for her in the Saloon and she looked around with interest at her fellow-passengers.

They did not seem to be very exciting and her thoughts drifted away into speculation of what lay ahead.

This was an adventure, something that a month ago she had never envisaged might happen.

Just for a moment, as she said goodbye to Nicky who had accompanied her to Dover, she felt a little panic-stricken.

It was with an effort that she stopped herself from pleading with him to take her home again, to say that she could not face going off alone into the unknown.

Then the courage she had never lacked, and the buoyancy that made her always believe everything would turn out for the best, made her bid her brother a tearless farewell.

Everything had happened so quickly and there had been so much to do before she left home that she had hardly had time to think of anything except getting her clothes together and preparing for the journey.

There had also been innumerable things to be packed and moved to the cottage where Lady Stanton was to live with Athene and Delos and also Cynthus until she married.

As her mother was inevitably helpless in such circumstances, Cynthus and Larisa found they had to do everything for her.

The decisions around Larisa's clothes had entailed a council of war and as usual she had the most sensible suggestions to make.

"As I am going abroad," she said, "where no-one will know me, there is no reason for me to wear mourning. Mama must obviously be in black for a year and a half's mourning. The rest of you will be expected to be sombrely garbed for nearly twelve months."

The others looked at her in surprise.

"And so, where I am concerned," Larisa said, "I can wear any colour that is available."

"What are you suggesting, dearest?" Lady Stanton asked in a bewildered voice.

"I am saying, Mama, that as we are all more or less the same size I will wear your clothes, especially your travelling gown and cloak, which will save a lot of money and time in making me one."

Before her mother could speak Larisa added quickly,

"I will be very careful of it and when you can wear colours again you can have it back."

"It is certainly an idea," Lady Stanton said slowly, "but at the same time my travelling gown and cloak are blue. What would people think?"

"People will think nothing," Larisa answered firmly, "first of all because they will not be interested in a governess and secondly, the *Comtesse* may not even have mentioned to her brother that Papa has only just died."

She looked at their surprised expressions and added,

"Anyway, if it makes you any happier, I will wear a black band around my arm."

"No, that looks horrible!" Cynthus said quickly. "I think Larisa has a good idea, Mama, and she can have my pink dress. It is my best but it will be out of fashion long before I can wear it again."

She paused to add,

"Besides I shall need new gowns for my trousseau."

"Of course you will, dearest," Lady Stanton agreed, "and somehow we will contrive some very pretty ones. You will look very attractive in mauves and lilacs, which are both considered to be half-mourning."

Larisa found quite a number of her mother's coloured clothes that could easily be altered to fit her and could be made to look a little younger in shape and design by her skilful fingers.

At the same time the evening gowns did look too old for her. Then Lady Stanton gave a little exclamation.

"I have an idea!"

"What is it, Mama?" Larisa asked.

"Ask Nicky to help you down with the trunk that is in the attic. The big brown leather one with the rounded top."

Lady Stanton sounded rather mysterious, and when the trunk was brought downstairs and opened, they were all intrigued by what it contained.

Lady Stanton, who had enjoyed a social success when she made her debut, had been the only child of a rich father.

He wanted the best for his daughter and was prepared to pay for it.

He had therefore taken her to London for the Season, where she had been invited to all the grand balls and she said, reminiscing, that she had been the *'belle'* of most of them!

Unfortunately, her father had decided that the financial future of the world lay in Australia.

He invested most of his money in gold shares and Lady Stanton's dowry, which on her marriage to Sir Beaugrave had been quite a considerable sum, was invested in a gold mine.

Five years later the mine dropped out of production and when her father died a few years later it was found that his very large fortune had vanished in Australian companies whose optimistic conjectures had never materialised.

"I kept some of my prettier gowns," Lady Stanton explained now, "simply as mementoes of my happy girlhood."

As she spoke, she drew from the trunk a whale-boned crinoline, which made her daughters collapse with laughter.

"Did you really wear that, Mama?" Athene asked. "It must have been very uncomfortable." "It was very inconvenient," Lady Stanton admitted, "and made it very difficult to get in and out of a carriage!"

She too laughed as she added,

"It was also very indecent if one sat down without thinking because it would shoot up in front revealing everything that was underneath!"

The gowns that went over the crinolines might, the girls thought, have been pretty when they were fashionable.

"This was my 'coming out' gown," Lady Stanton explained.

She held up a creation of white satin trimmed around the off-the-shoulder bodice with shadow lace, which also decorated the full skirt.

"It is nice material," Athene said.

"It was very expensive," Lady Stanton answered.

"I suppose we could alter it?" Larisa suggested doubtfully.

"Put it on," Lady Stanton said.

Larisa did as her mother suggested. The bodice, which revealed the perfect curves of her small breasts, was certainly becoming.

But she looked down in dismay at the limp satin skirt drooping over the floor as there was no crinoline to make it stand out.

Then Lady Stanton swept it backwards.

"If we moulded it in the front to your figure," she said, "the rest would drape at the back into a pretty train."

Larisa gave a cry of delight.

"Of course it would! How clever of you, Mama!"

There was another gown in the trunk. It was sky-blue crepe trimmed with tulle, which they felt would respond to the same treatment.

There were also several pairs of white kid gloves fitting at the wrist, little flower-wreaths, which Athene appropriated because they were so pretty, and a fan from which Delos refused to be parted.

"I thought I had more things," Lady Stanton said regretfully, "but I remember now I made one gown into a cloak for Athene's Christening and several more into your party dresses as children, when I did not like to ask your Papa for money to buy new ones."

"These two gowns will do me beautifully,' Larisa said, "except that I suspect they will be far too smart for a governess!"

She was quite certain that that was true when they were finished.

They all helped with the sewing, stitching, pressing and arranging until, when finally the gowns were finished and Larisa tried them on, Cynthus was quite jealous.

"I am sure they ought to be in my trousseau," she said. "I will never be able to afford anything half as beautiful!"

"I have the feeling," Larisa said looking at herself in the mirror, "that I shall never wear these gowns. So I will wrap them in paper and keep them very carefully and when you get married you shall have them!"

That is sweet of you, Larisa!" Cynthus said and kissed her.

The blue dress was not as elaborate as the white when it was finished, but it still looked very striking when Larisa wore it.

"You look as if you were stepping out of a sunlit sky!" Cynthus said poetically.

"I think the only person who will wear this gown will be you!" Larisa replied, "unless I put it on to eat a frugal meal by myself, which will be brought up to me on a tray to the schoolroom."

Lady Stanton looked at her daughter in astonishment.

"Do you not think they expect you to eat in the dining room, Larisa?" she enquired.

"I think it most unlikely, Mama. You know Papa would never have Miss Grimshaw or Miss Johnson downstairs for dinner, and they only had luncheon with you because we were there also."

"I had forgotten," Lady Stanton said. "It is so long ago. Oh, Larisa, I cannot bear to think of your being treated in such a manner! What would your Papa think?"

"Papa might have thought of that when he was buying all those expensive books." Larisa said in a hard voice. "I only hope Nicky gets some of the money back on them, but now of course they are second-hand and perhaps no one will want them."

She had in fact been shocked by her father's extravagance when she and Nicky had finished sorting through the library.

It was easy to see where so much of his capital had been expended year after year.

"I wonder why he loved Greece so much?" she had remarked to her brother.

"He thought of nothing else," Nicky said. "I suppose if he had followed his inclinations, he would have left us all and gone to live there."

"Perhaps he had been Greek in a past existence," Larisa said dreamily.

"Do you believe in such things?" her brother enquired.

"I have often thought about it," Larisa answered. "It is hard to understand, without believing in some form of reincarnation, why one child can show an amazing aptitude at a very early age for music, or another like Delos could speak French almost before she was proficient at English!"

"That is obviously an inheritance from our great-grandmother," Nicky said.

"Is it?" Larisa asked, "or is there a different explanation?"

Her brother smiled.

"Perhaps I have been an Ambassador in another life," he said. "That is why I am so keen to go into the Diplomatic Service!"

"And you will be an Ambassador again, I am sure of it!" Larisa smiled. "Think how handsome you will look with all that gold embroidery on your uniform."

Nicky laughed and they had gone on sorting out the books that were to be sold.

But every day as they packed up the big family house, Larisa found it harder to understand how her father could have been so imprudent.

Now aboard the *Britannia,* Larisa told herself that if it had not been for Sir Beaugrave's obsession with Greece she would not at this moment be setting out on what she was sure would be a sort of adventure for which she had often longed.

'I shall see France,' she told herself, 'I shall meet French people and if it is too unpleasant or difficult I can always go home.'

It was a nice, cosy feeling to think that she could always return to Mama, Athene and Delos.

Anyway she would do her best to stay at least until Nicky had completed his studies at Oxford.

She and Nicky had been obliged to stay the night in Dover so that Larisa could catch the early boat to Calais.

They had put up at a cheap and not very comfortable hotel, but at least they had been together.

They had laughed at the other people staying there and Larisa had enjoyed every moment of the rather unpalatable supper because Nicky was with her.

"You will look after yourself, Larisa?" he said when they had finished eating.

"You know I shall," she replied, "and if any of us had to go abroad it is best that it should be me!"

"Why do you say that?" he enquired.

"Cynthus has always been rather vague. I feel that if she was looking after a child she would forget about him if she was reading a book or lost in one of her daydreams. Athene is far too impulsive and Delos is too romantic!"

Nicky laughed.

"And I suppose you are none of those things?"

"I am full of common sense. At least I hope so!"

"I am not sure about that, but I have always thought that you are the cleverest of my sisters, and perhaps the bravest!"

Larisa looked at him with deep affection.

"Do you mean that?"

"I mean it," he said, "but I am going to worry about you, Larisa. You are far too pretty to be let loose alone on the Continent. I am quite sure there are going to be a lot of Frenchmen to tell you so!"

"I promised to Mama not to listen to the smallest compliment!"

Nicky laughed again, but it was rather ruefully.

"Poor Mama. She has no idea of what the world is like outside Redmarley House and quite frankly, Larisa, it is not going to be easy for you."

"I know that," Larisa said in a serious tone. "At the same time, you are all there just across the sea and if things get too difficult, I shall just come home."

"You do that," Nicky said.

He was silent for a moment and then he added,

"It is awfully hard for me to know how to say thank you for what you are doing for me."

"Now you are making me feel embarrassed," Larisa protested. "We love you, Nicky, and I know you would do the same for us if it was the other way around."

"You know I would," he answered.

'£150 a year!' Larisa thought to herself as the steamer puffed its way across a comparatively calm sea.

It seemed an enormous amount of money for teaching a small child how to speak English, and she wondered what would happen if the boy did not learn as quickly as his grandfather expected him to do.

She was sure however, that French children were quick-witted, and it would not be as difficult for him to learn English as it would be for an English child to learn French.

The steamer arrived at Calais on time and the train to Paris was waiting in the station.

A porter at the quayside placed Larisa's trunk in the van and carried her holdall along the train until he found a Second-Class carriage inscribed 'Ladies only'.

He helped her into it, and she settled herself in a window seat so that she could see as much of the countryside as possible.

The carriage was empty when she entered but a few minutes later the door was opened and a lady climbed in.

She was very elaborately gowned in what seemed to Larisa to be an exaggerated version of the fashions she and the family had pored over in *The Ladies Journal*.

There was an expensive exotic fragrance about her as she moved into the seat opposite Larisa.

A porter carried in an enormous number of packages, which he stowed away in the rack over her head.

The lady tipped him and as he said, *"Merci beaucoup, Madame!"*, Larisa knew it had been a generous *pourboire*.

The lady settled herself down, her skirts rustling over silk petticoats. Her jacket was trimmed with a fur, which Larisa thought might be sable. There was a diamond brooch at her throat.

It seemed much warmer than it had been in the Channel and after a few moments the lady took off her fur-trimmed jacket.

Larisa saw that underneath it her gown was elaborately fashioned with lace inset at the neck in an intricate style that she knew she could never attempt to copy.

The train started off after much blowing of a whistle, and a clashing of couplings and buffers that made the carriage rock.

Black smoke from the engine blew past the windows, which were fortunately closed.

Larisa stared out as they passed the ugly buildings that bordered the quayside, continued past a few suburban houses then reached the open countryside.

This was what she had wanted to see, the broad acres of France, the poplars bordering the roads, the farmers working in the fields.

It was as they gathered speed that one of the packages belonging to the other occupant of the compartment fell down from the rack.

The lady gave an exclamation of annoyance and, looking up, Larisa realised that quite a number of the other packages were likely to fall if nothing was done about them.

"Let me assist you, *Madame*!" she exclaimed in French.

"Merci bien!" the lady replied.

Larisa climbed onto the seat and, holding herself steady with one hand on the rack she managed to secure the rest of the packages, adjusting them so that there was no likelihood of any more falling on their owner's head.

"The porter was an imbecile to place my things so precariously!" the lady said.

"They will be safe now," Larisa answered.

She stepped down from the seat on which she had been standing and sat down.

"It is very kind of you, *Mademoiselle*, to help me," the lady said, glancing at her ringless hand as she spoke.

"It is a pleasure, *Madame*," Larisa replied politely.

"You are English?"

"Yes, I have just crossed the Channel."

"That is what I thought – and is this your first visit to France?"

"My first," Larisa admitted.

"I hope you will enjoy it," the lady said.

Then she smiled.

"I think there could be no doubt about that! You are very pretty, *Mademoiselle!*"

"Thank you," Larisa answered.

"And your gown becomes you. Where was it made?"

Larisa was so surprised at the question that for a moment she did not reply and the lady said quickly,

"Forgive me! You will think it an impertinence, but I must explain. I am Madame Madeleine."

Larisa was wondering what she should reply to this when the lady went on,

"I forget that means nothing to you, but it is a name of some importance in Paris. I am not Monsieur Worth, you understand, but I am still a dressmaker of the *haute couture.*"

"A dressmaker!" Larisa exclaimed.

Without meaning to she glanced at the many packages that she had been re-arranging on the rack.

"Exactly!" the lady said with a smile. "I have been to London after visiting the North of France to buy lace for the gowns I design."

She saw that Larisa was interested and went on,

"There are no lace-makers as skilful as those in Normandy and Brittany. They work in their homes and many of them cannot read, so it is impossible for them to send what they make to Paris."

She made a gesture with her hand as she continued,

"*Voyons,* I therefore have to visit them myself and explain while I am there my requirements for next year."

"I understand," Larisa said. "Is it easy to make lace?"

She wondered as she spoke whether she could learn to make it.

"It is an art that has been handed down from generation to generation," Madame Madeleine replied. "Very often one family will have a secret design, which they prize jealously and must not be copied."

"It sounds fascinating!" Larisa exclaimed.

"The lace is also very decorative," Madame Madeleine answered, "and because it is hand-made I can charge a very high price for it when it is on one of my gowns."

She smiled and added,

"Now you will understand why I asked you where your gown was made."

"It belonged to my mother," Larisa said frankly, "and she bought it in London some years ago."

"The colour is perfect with your skin," Madame Madeleine said. "But then, *Mademoiselle,* almost anything you wore would become you. I hope one day I may have the pleasure of dressing you."

Larisa laughed.

"I am afraid that is something which will never happen, *Madame!* Although it would be exciting to think it might!"

"Why are you so sure?" Madame Madeleine asked. "With your looks, beautiful and expensive gowns should be easily obtainable!"

"For a governess?" Larisa asked. "No, I must make my own dresses – when I can afford the material!"

"You are a governess?" Madame exclaimed.

"That is why I have come to France," Larisa answered. "I am to teach a little boy to speak English."

"But such a position is a waste of your beauty!" Madame protested.

"I am very fortunate in getting this position," Larisa said seriously. "You see, most people want much older governesses."

"And not such pretty ones!" Madame said and added, "I can understand that. At the same time, it seems a sad waste."

"Waste?" Larisa queried, thinking that perhaps she had misunderstood the word.

"With your looks you could be a sensation on the stage or wherever the gentlemen of Paris could – see you."

Larisa laughed.

"If my mother could hear you, she would faint. She would die rather than allow me to go on the stage! Besides I doubt if I have the talent for acting."

Madame Madeleine looked at her sharply as if she suspected Larisa of being sarcastic. Then she asked,

"How old are you, *Mademoiselle,* if you do not think it rude of me to question you?"

"I am eighteen," Larisa replied, "but I am trying to look older so that people will not think I am too young to teach."

"I do not think it is your age that will worry them," Madame said quietly noting Larisa's golden hair, wide blue eyes and small, classical features.

Then she said in a more conversational tone,

"Will you be living in Paris?"

"No indeed," Larisa answered. "I am going to Valmont-sur-Seine."

Madame Madeleine did not speak and Larisa added a little proudly,

"I am to teach the grandson of Le Comte de Valmont!"

Madame Madeleine sat up sharply.

"Le Comte de Valmont?" she repeated, *"C'est impossible!"*

"Why is it impossible?" Larisa asked.

"To go to the *Château* Valmont? No, *M'mselle!* No! No! *No!"*

"Why do you say that?" Larisa asked. "Is there something wrong?"

"It depends what you mean by wrong," Madame Madeleine replied, "but if you meet Comte Raoul de Valmont it would be a catastrophe!"

Larisa looked at her in perplexity.

"Who is the Comte Raoul?"

"You have not heard of him?"

"No, never!" Larisa answered. "It was the Comte de Valmont who wrote to my mother, and he signed his name 'Francois'."

"He is head of the family," Madame Madeleine explained. "He is a great aristocrat. The de Valmonts are part of the history of France."

"Then why do you speak in such a way of Comte Raoul, whoever he may be?" Larisa enquired.

"Perhaps you will not see him," Madame Madeleine said almost as if she spoke to herself. "He is always in Paris. They say he does not get on with his father, and who would be surprised at that?"

"What are you talking about?" Larisa asked. "Please explain. You must realise it is important to me?"

"If you were my daughter," Madame Madeleine replied, "I would put you on the first ship sailing from Calais to Dover and send you home."

"But why? *Why?*" Larisa insisted.

Because, *pauvre petite,*" Madame Madeleine said, "Comte Raoul is not for such as you!"

"I cannot quite understand what he has to do with it," Larisa said.

"He is of course the father of the little boy you will be teaching," Madame replied.

"I had not realised that Jean-Pierre had a father!" Larisa exclaimed. "When his grandfather wrote to Mama, she thought – in fact we all thought – that the little boy must be an orphan."

"He has a father," Madame Madeleine said. "A father who, I assure you, *Mademoiselle,* no-one could ignore. And yet you may not see him. People are always gossiping about Comte Raoul, and if rumour is to be believed he and his father are always at each other's throats!"

"Why should they talk about him?" Larisa asked.

"Because, *Mademoiselle,* he is most dashing, the most sought-after, the most sensational young man in all Paris!"

Madame Madeleine drew in her breath before she went on,

"Everyone talks about him. All the women run after him! *'Monsieur le Diable'* is what they call him, and I can assure you that the name is apt."

"Why? What does he do to deserve such a nickname?"

"He tempts every woman that he meets into indiscretion and folly," Madame Madeleine replied. "Ah, *Mademoiselle,* if you only knew how easily they yield to him."

Madame Madeleine threw out her hands in an expressive gesture.

"*'Vite! Vite! Madame,"* they say to me. "Your best gown, your smartest, your most exquisite! Tonight, I must look alluring, beautiful, different. I must outshine everybody."

Madame Madeleine gave a little laugh.

"I do not even have to ask why. I know it is because they are dining with Comte Raoul!"

"Why is he so attractive to them?" Larisa enquired.

"Who can explain why such a man can make every woman he meets fall wildly in love with him?" Madame Madeleine enquired. "She may be a Duchess – a *Grande Dame* who moves in only the very best circles – she may be the star of the Folies Bergères or the Moulin Rouge. She may be in the theatre or in some *Café Chantant*. Wherever there is an attractive woman, Comte Raoul will find her and when he finds her – *Voyons!* she is lost!"

Larisa's eyes were on Madame Madeleine's face.

It was obvious she was fascinated by what she was being told.

"And does the Comte fall in love with them?" she asked.

Madame Madeleine shrugged.

"What is love?" she asked. "Is it the nectar a man finds in every flower he touches with his lips? Or is it the excitement of knowing that he has only to snap his fingers and they run at his bidding?"

"And has Comte Raoul a wife?" Larisa asked.

"No, no. She is dead!" Madame Madeleine replied. "She was the mother of the little boy you will be teaching, and she died in childbirth."

"That was sad for him," Larisa said.

Again, Madame Madeleine shrugged.

"If he is unhappy, he showed no sign of it," she said. "His parties are stupendous! All Paris talks about them and all Paris fights to be invited. That is – feminine Paris!"

"Then men do not like the wicked *Comte*?" Larisa asked.

"Now it is rather strange that you should say that, *Mademoiselle*," Madame Madeleine answered, "because if most men behaved in such a scandalous manner other men would ostracise him or he would have to fight too many duels to survive. But the *Comte* is popular with his own sex."

"They are not jealous of him?" Larisa asked.

"If they are jealous, then it is because he is what they would like to be!" Madame Madeleine replied. "Old men admire his sportsmanship and his successes on the racecourse as well as on the dance floor. It makes them recall their youth."

She smiled.

"To the *Comte's* contemporaries he is someone to envy, to copy and to rival – even if they fail."

Larisa was silent for a moment and then she said,

"You say the *Comte* has quarrelled with his father. This means that if he does not visit the *Château* I shall be unlikely to see him."

"Let us hope that is so, *Mademoiselle,*" Madame Madeleine said. "As I have already said, it would be a disaster for the *Comte* to set eyes on you!"

"But why?" Larisa enquired.

"Look in the mirror, *Mademoiselle.*"

Larisa laughed.

"Now you are flattering me," she said. "If the *Comte* has all the sophisticated and elegant women in Paris running after him, then he is unlikely to look at a governess."

Madame Madeleine gave a little sigh.

"Let us hope that is the truth," she said, "and yet, *ma petite,* I am worried on your behalf."

"It is very kind of you, *Madame*, but I assure you I can look after myself," Larisa said. "My mother has already warned me that when Frenchmen pay compliments it means nothing and I have promised her not to listen to them."

Madame Madeleine shook her head.

"So self-confident!" she sighed. "So young! I remember feeling like that when I was your age which is unfortunately more years ago than I care to remember!"

"But you have been a great success, *Madame*!" Larisa said.

"With a little help from – friends," Madame Madeleine replied with a pause before the last word. "And quite a lot of heartaches on the way."

"You have been unhappy?" Larisa asked sympathetically."

"I think women are brought into the world to be unhappy," Madame Madeleine said. "If you are pretty, you walk the dangerous path with pitfalls on either side of it – and if you are plain there are no pitfalls but you weep bitter tears of frustration!"

Larisa laughed. She could not help it.

"Oh, *Madame*, you make it sound so gloomy. I always believed that Paris was very exciting."

"It is, in the Paris that you will not see."

"Tell me about the parties Comte Raoul gives," Larisa urged.

"You are curious, *Mademoiselle*. That is a mistake!" Madame exclaimed.

But she was an inveterate gossip and Larisa soon persuaded her to tell her what she wished to hear.

"Once the *Comte* wagered an epicure the sum of 50 thousand francs," *Madame* began, "that he would find him a dinner at which the main course would be the most delicious and delectable meat in Paris but he would not wish to eat it."

"The epicure accepted the wager?" Larisa asked.

"He did – and lost!"

"How?"

"The fish dishes were superb. Then the *entrée* was brought into the dining room on a huge silver dish."

Madame paused.

"Inside was Fifi le Fleur – the star of the *Folies Bergères*, stark naked!"

Larisa laughed even though she was shocked.

"On another occasion," *Madame* continued, "one of the *Comte's* guests danced a fandango on the table at *Maxim*s, which is the smartest restaurant patronised by the *beau monde* and the *demi-monde*. She caused a sensation!"

"It sounds full of gaiety," Larisa exclaimed, wondering who the *demi-monde* were.

"There is gaiety and gaiety," Madame Madeleine said gravely, "and you, *Mademoiselle*, must be careful you do not become involved in the wrong sort."

"How shall I know the wrong from the right?" Larisa asked.

"Avoid the temptations of the devil!" Madame Madeleine said impressively, "and that is Comte Raoul!"

*

The carriage that awaited Larisa at the *Gare du Nord* was drawn by two fine horses.

An aged retainer in black and gold livery with crested buttons who met her at the platform apologised that the *Comte* had not sent a courier for her.

"Monsieur Le Comte regrets, *M'mselle,*" he said, "that the relative who often obliges him in such duties is indisposed. There is however a maid to attend you."

"Thank you," Larisa replied.

When she climbed into the carriage, she found a woman neatly dressed in black on the seat with her back to the horses.

"Bonjour, M'mselle"

"Bonjour!" Larisa replied.

The trunks were secured outside and the retainer climbed up on the box beside the coachman. The horses started off and they moved out of the station.

It was getting late and the gaslights were already lit. Larisa leant forward to stare excitedly at the tall grey houses with their wooden shutters, at shops lit up and still doing business, at the cafés with their customers seated outside on the pavement, at marble-topped tables on which stood glasses of wine.

"I have been looking forward to seeing Paris," she said to the elderly maid.

"It is very crowded and noisy, *M'mselle.*"

"You prefer the country?"

"I have always lived at Valmont-sur-Seine."

"You have not found it dull?" Larisa asked.

"No, *M'mselle,* I've been grateful that I could work in such pleasant surroundings."

There seemed to be little more to gain from this conversation and Larisa stared out of the window without speaking.

She had taken the trouble to find out a lot about Paris before she left England.

She knew that the gigantic International Exhibition of the previous year 1889 had impressed the world.

"The fact that the Exhibition was held on the centenary of the year of the Revolution was not to everyone's taste," Nicky told her.

He was always full of information on anything that concerned diplomacy.

"None of the Royal Courts of Europe were represented by their Ambassadors," he continued, "with the exception of Belgium."

"What about England?" Larisa asked.

"Queen Victoria recalled our Ambassador, Lord Lytton, to London," Nicky replied, "so that he did not have to be present at the opening ceremony."

"But was it a success?"

"Over thirty-two million attendances were registered during the Exhibition," Nicky answered, "and when he visited Paris the Prince of Wales climbed to the top of the Eiffel Tower."

"That is what I want to do!" Larisa exclaimed.

"A lot of people have predicted it will collapse!"

"I will risk it," Larisa laughed.

From the books she read she learnt that Paris had doubled in size since the beginning of the century.

The city had also been transformed by Napoleon III and Baron Haussmann who had cut through its centuries-old maze of houses, streets and alleys with broad new boulevards.

"I want to see the *Rue de Rivoli* and the *Champs Élysées*," Larisa told Nicky.

"I would rather go to the *Folies Bergères* and *Maxims*," he grinned.

"Tell me about them." Larisa begged.

"They are not for young ladies," he teased, "and most especially not for prim, precise, proper young governesses."

She threw a cushion at him.

Now she had heard more about the *Folies Bergères* and *Maxims* she thought, and Nicky was right, they were not places she could ever visit.

She had also been intrigued, if shocked, by Madame Madeleine's revelations about Le Comte Raoul.

At the same time she felt certain that *Madame*, who was extremely voluble had exaggerated.

She could not help feeling that if Comte Raoul was as notoriously bad as he was made out to be, Lady Luddington would not have recommended her for the position. At the same time the Comtesse de Chalon would not expect her nephew to be interested in a mere Governess when, as Madame Madeleine had said, all the most beautiful women in Paris were throwing themselves at his feet.

'I wonder what he is really like?' Larisa thought to herself.

She had known so few men and those who had come to Redmarley House or had partnered her at the few balls that she had attended had certainly not behaved like devils, nor had they been so alluringly attractive that she had ever troubled to think of them again.

She tried to think of what she thought would be most exciting and desirable in a man or indeed what, the dream-man who at times she had imagined she might marry, would look like.

It was hard to express in words the sort of man she wanted as a husband. Certainly not someone like the young man Cynthus was to marry.

It was something she would never have said to her sister, but Larisa found John Pirbank extremely boring.

There was certainly nothing wrong with him. He was good-looking in an unobtrusive manner and he was well bred. He rode comparatively well and he had a sense of duty, which was entirely commendable.

Because his father did not wish him to marry too young, he was prepared to agree that he and Cynthus should wait another year before their engagement was to be announced.

Larisa had often thought that she would be rather piqued if someone who loved her was prepared to accept that their future should be arranged by his father and that he himself did not kick against the lengthy interval that must elapse before they could be married.

'Cynthus is happy!' Larisa told herself. 'At the same time, I would want a man who was more spirited, more forceful – and who would perhaps be a little more authoritative about his own life!'

Now she told herself sitting back against the soft cushions of the carriage that she certainly did not want anyone like Comte Raoul.

To have dozens of rivals for one's husband's affections would, she felt, be to invite all the heartaches of which Madame Madeleine had spoken.

Then puckishly a question came to her as to whether it was more upsetting to have as a rival a man's absorbing interest like her father's had been with Greece, or for it to be another woman.

'I wonder which Papa really loved the best,' she asked herself, 'Greece or Mama?'

Then she told herself she was being absurd.

Her father and mother had been very happy. There was no doubt about that.

Lady Stanton had admired her husband, and while at times it had seemed Sir Beaugrave lived in another world and to be barely conscious that his family was there, he had undoubtedly been a contented man.

'Why am I thinking about him?' Larisa chided herself as they drove on through the gathering darkness.

Because she wished to force herself to concentrate on the life that lay ahead of her, she asked the elderly woman,

"Has the little boy had any lessons so far?"

"He has had several governesses, *M'mselle*"

"Several?" Larisa questioned in surprise.

"Yes, *M'mselle*"

"Then why have they left?"

The question was out before Larisa could prevent it.

Even as she spoke, she knew it was something she should not ask, as it might seem that she was gossiping with a servant. But the reply came quickly.

"They did not teach Monsieur Jean-Pierre to the satisfaction of Monsieur Le Comte."

'That was that!' Larisa thought and if she was not satisfactory one thing was obvious, she would soon be returning to the *Gare du Nord* and back across the Channel.

For the first time she felt nervous not at being on her own but because it would be so humiliating to be dismissed as incompetent.

What had Jean-Pierre's other governesses been like? Why had they not been successful?

She longed to ask more questions, but even as they rose to her lips she knew it would be most indiscreet and unladylike for her to ask them.

She must wait and see what happened when she arrived and above all things she must be confident and sure of herself.

There was however one thing she must ask.

"Is *le petit Monsieur* a good little boy?"

"Very good, *M'mselle*. He's no trouble," was the answer.

If that was so, Larisa thought to herself, what could be the difficulty?

Why had the other governesses not been able to please Monsieur le Comte?

She thought again of all the things Madame Madeleine had told her.

She had never had a very clear picture in her mind of what *Château* Valmont would be like, but it was certainly going to be different from what she had expected.

Perhaps different in every way from anything she might have encountered had she become a governess in England.

Without including the possibility of meeting Comte Raoul, the notorious *Monsieur le Diable!*

CHAPTER THREE

It was growing dark when they approached the *Château* but as the carriage drove down a long drive lined with lime trees, Larisa could see the outline of a huge building.

As she drew nearer still she realised that the *Château* itself was surrounded by a wide moat and the bridge spanning it was surmounted by exquisitely carved statues.

There was however no time for her to see anything clearly.

The carriage crossed the bridge and drew up with a flourish in a courtyard where light came streaming from a great door set on top of a long flight of steps.

"We have arrived, *M'mselle*" the old maid remarked unnecessarily.

A footman opened the carriage door, Larisa stepped out and walked up the steps.

She felt rather small and frightened as she entered a huge hall, circular in shape with pillars and alcoves in which there were busts.

The butler who had bowed to her on her arrival indicated the stairs, which curved upwards, and a footman preceded her leading her to the first landing.

Here she was met by a woman whom she imagined to be the housekeeper, dressed in black with a silk apron. She was an elderly woman, with an austere expression.

"Good evening, *M'mselle*," she said. "I will take you to Madame Savigny."

Larisa remembered that this was the name of the widowed sister of the *Comte* who the Comtesse de Chalon had said would be living in the *Château*.

She followed the housekeeper down a long corridor decorated with portraits of ugly, bewigged gentlemen whom Larisa guessed were Valmont ancestors.

The housekeeper knocked at a door and when a quiet voice said *"entrez"* she announced,

"*M'mselle* Stanton has just arrived, *Madame.*"

Larisa entering saw it was a private sitting room filled with what were obviously an old lady's treasures.

There was a parrot in a cage, a marquetry work-box open beside an armchair, innumerable small *objets d'art* of no particular value but which were obviously kept for sentimental reasons, and a profusion of water colours.

Set upon tables or arranged on small easels, everywhere one looked the eye encountered them.

Sitting in an armchair was an elderly lady who Larisa thought at once was exactly what a French aristocrat should look like.

She had a high-bridged, pointed nose and a long neck and her grey hair was swept back from her forehead under a lace cap.

There was a cameo brooch at the neck of her black dress and on her blue-veined, but rather trembling old hands, there were a number of brilliant rings.

Larisa advanced towards her, realising as she did so that Madame Savigny's eyes were regarding her with little expression save one of indifference.

There was a smile on her pale lips and she waited until Larisa curtsied before she said,

"You are late, Miss Stanton!"

"The steamer was on time at Calais, *Madame*," Larisa answered, "but I fancied the train was late coming into the *Gare du Nord*."

Madame Savigny inclined her head as if she accepted the explanation.

"You speak French well."

"Thank you, *Madame*."

She did not invite Larisa to sit down and she therefore stood feeling perhaps that she looked a little untidy after the long journey, and conscious for the first time of being tired.

"Monsieur Le Comte will wish to see you after you have changed," Madame Savigny said, "and there will be something for you to eat in the schoolroom. The housekeeper will show you the way."

"Thank you, *Madame*."

Larisa realised that she was dismissed.

She curtsied again and found that the housekeeper was waiting at the door.

Once again, they walked some distance down long passages and then climbed by what was obviously a back staircase to the second floor.

Here another woman was waiting for her, more elderly than the housekeeper or Madame Savigny.

This, *M'mselle*," the housekeeper, announced, "is Nurse, who looks after *le petit Monsieur*."

"*Bonsoir!*" Larisa said holding out her hand.

After a moment's hesitation the nurse took it and again Larisa thought there was no welcome in her eyes and there was certainly no smile on her lips.

"Will you come this way?" Nurse asked.

Larisa turned to the housekeeper and said,

"Thank you very much for looking after me."

She thought for a moment the woman seemed surprised at her courtesy.

She followed the nurse to an open door and entered what she knew was the schoolroom.

It had obviously originally been a nursery. There was the high fireguard, the screen, the table in the centre of the room and the rocking horse that made it a prototype of nurseries in every country all over the world. But as a concession to Jean-Pierre's advanced years there was a blackboard, a child's small desk, and a large map of Europe suspended on the wall.

"I expect the little boy is asleep at this time of the night," Larisa said.

"He goes to bed at 6 o'clock," the nurse answered.

"Just as I was made to do at that age!" Larisa smiled.

"It always seemed too early in the summertime."

Just for a moment she thought there was a flicker of a smile in the old woman's eyes before she replied,

"It's important for him to have plenty of sleep."

"Yes, of course," Larisa agreed.

Nurse indicated a room that was one of two leading out of the nursery.

"Jean-Pierre is in there," she said. "I am next door. I have always slept there and I see no reason for change."

She spoke truculently, and Larisa guessed that this had been a bone of contention with other governesses.

"I have no wish to make any changes as to where Jean-Pierre or you sleep," she said quickly. "All I am concerned with is teaching him, and I am sure he would much rather have you near him at night."

"I'll show you to your room, *M'mselle*," the nurse said.

This proved to be just across the passage and was a small, pleasant room that looked out over the front of the *Château*.

Larisa had an idea that it would have a magnificent view, but for the moment it was too dark to see anything clearly.

While she had been in the schoolroom with Nurse two footmen had carried up her trunks.

Now they were set down in the centre of the room.

"Suzanne will help you to unpack," Nurse said.

"I can manage by myself if she is busy," Larisa replied, then asked, "Who is Suzanne?"

"She is a schoolroom maid," Nurse answered. "At this moment she will be fetching your supper from downstairs. As soon as she has brought it into the schoolroom she will let you know."

"Thank you very much."

Larisa paused a moment and then she added,

"I hope, Nurse, that you will help me. This is my first position. I am very anxious to do what is right and of course I am afraid of making mistakes."

Nurse looked at her sharply. Then suddenly her hostility vanished as she said,

"You're very young, *M'mselle*. We were expecting someone older."

"So will you tell me what to do," Larisa asked pleadingly.

"Monsieur le Comte will do that," Nurse answered in a different tone of voice to what she had used before, "but

~61~

don't be too frightened of him, *M'mselle*. He only wants what is best for his grandson."

"He is fond of him?" Larisa asked.

"Jean-Pierre is the apple of his eye," the nurse replied. "But he asks too much of a small boy. That's what I say, but he'll not listen to me. He asks too much!"

As Nurse was speaking, she opened Larisa's trunk.

The footmen had undone the straps and now she began to take out Larisa's gowns and carry them to the wardrobe.

"What shall I wear to meet Monsieur le Comte?" Larisa asked and she thought that Nurse looked pleased because she sounded helpless.

"Nothing too elaborate," she answered. "In fact something simple. I imagine *Monsieur* also is expecting someone older."

"I see that I must convince Monsieur le Comte that I am a good teacher," Larisa said. "Surely that is what is important, not whether one is old or young?"

"The previous old ones were certainly quite useless!" Nurse said and now there was a touch of venom in her voice. "Coming here, giving their orders, pushing people around! Not one of them has lasted long! It's not surprising if the child has learnt nothing!"

"Oh dear!" Larisa said, "I hope I can succeed where they have failed!"

"Now don't you worry yourself, *M'mselle*," Nurse said in a motherly tone. "Wash and put on one of these pretty gowns, and when you have had something to eat, I'll tell Suzanne to go downstairs and say you are ready for when Monsieur le Comte can see you."

Larisa felt almost as if she were still a child herself as she obeyed.

Nurse was so like her own nanny who had looked after them all since Nicky had been born, that she found herself chatting away quite naturally.

She told the old woman how much the schoolroom was like the one they had at home and how their own nurse still thought of them as being under her care, and quite incapable of doing anything without her help.

"How many years have you been at the *Château*?" Larisa asked.

"Forty!" Nurse replied. "I came when I was a girl to work in the house. Then when Madame la Comtesse required an extra lady's maid, I helped look after her. She took a fancy to me, so when Monsieur Raoul was born I helped her old nurse who was almost on her last legs to look after the baby."

Nurse sighed.

"And what a beautiful baby he was. When the old nurse died, I had him all to myself."

"He was a good baby?"

"Yes, but he grew into a regular little pickle! But then he twisted me round his little finger, I could refuse him nothing."

'Like all the women he was to know later!' Larisa thought.

She found her interest quicken at the mention of Monsieur Raoul but she thought it unwise to ask too many questions.

She had the feeling that having broken the ice where the nurse was concerned she would hear in time the answers to all her questions without appearing curious.

The supper awaiting her in the schoolroom was served on small silver dishes and was delicious.

"You'll have to let Chef know tomorrow what your preferences are," Nurse said. "He's very obliging, but the last governesses drove him to distraction, poor man! One could not eat cheese, another mushrooms, a third one nothing cooked with eggs – there was no pleasing them!"

"I eat everything!" Larisa said, "and if every meal is as good as this I shall get so fat that I shall have to let out all my gowns!"

Nurse seemed pleased at her appreciation.

She would have withdrawn politely while Larisa ate but instead Larisa indicated a chair at the table and said,

"Please sit down and talk to me. There is so much I want to hear."

Nurse looked surprised and she added,

"Unless of course you are waiting for your own supper?"

"No indeed," the nurse answered, "we have ours later after the dining room has finished."

"The dining room are eating now?" Larisa enquired.

Nurse nodded.

"Then Monsieur le Comte will not be sending for me until after he has finished," Larisa said, "so do please stay with me."

She saw that the old nurse was pleased with the invitation and guessed that previous governesses had tried to prove themselves very superior from the moment of their arrival.

Having had a nurse of her own for so many years, Larisa was well aware how easy it was for a newcomer to cause umbrage or to encroach on privileges that had become traditional.

Looking back, she could remember when they had governesses before her father had got rid of them. There had been an endless battle between the schoolroom and the nursery.

She had the feeling that perhaps Nurse would be her only friend in the *Château*.

Already she was feeling slightly depressed by Madame Savigny's attitude and what she had been told about her predecessors, so she was ready to cling to her not only for the sake of peace but because she genuinely needed her help.

"Tell me about Jean-Pierre," she asked when she had finished her supper.

Suzanne had brought a pot of coffee, which she had set down on a table after she had removed the tray.

"He's a happy child," Nurse replied.

"He must find it rather lonely here, or are there other children with whom he can play?" Larisa asked.

"He's quite content," Nurse said quickly.

Larisa made a note that the suggestion of companions might be a tricky subject. Then she said tentatively,

"He must miss having a brother, but perhaps he sees a lot of his father?"

She knew this was a pertinent question and she fancied that the nurse hesitated before she said,

"What a child doesn't have he doesn't miss! Jean-Pierre is happy enough if people do not try to push him into doing things of which he is not capable."

She spoke almost sharply, and Larisa realised that her question about Jean-Pierre's father had remained unanswered. There were so many more things she wanted to know, but before she could work Nurse round to answering the right questions the summons came for her to meet Monsieur le Comte.

A footman brought the message.

"Monsieur le Comte asks if *M'mselle* will descend immediately to the salon."

The order sounded rather awe-inspiring and Larisa glanced at Nurse as she rose from the table.

"Don't be frightened," Nurse said to her in a quiet voice that only she could hear. "Remember he loves the child."

Nevertheless, Larisa could not help feeling nervous as she followed the footman down two flights of stairs to the doors until they reached the ground floor.

They walked along wide and well-proportioned corridors until they reached two large doors painted and gilded in the exquisite fashion of the 18th century.

The footman pulled them open and Larisa entered one of the most impressive salons she had ever seen.

It was nearly square with long windows covered with hand-embroidered curtains.

The carved gilt panels on the walls were surmounted by a ceiling that was painted with a profusion of goddesses and cupids.

There was an Aubusson carpet on the floor and the gilt and damask sofa and chairs were of the reign of Louis XIV. The other furniture of the same period would have delighted any connoisseur and the commodes with their marble tops and ornate handles were the finest she had ever seen outside a picture-book.

She only had a very quick impression of the room, for her interest was focused on a man sitting at a flat-topped rosewood desk in the centre of it.

The high back of the carved chair behind him was a frame for one of the most distinguished-looking old men Larisa had ever seen.

He looked, she thought to herself, intimidating yet awe-inspiring and autocratic, but at the same time he had a presence that one could not help admiring.

Feeling rather like a schoolgirl about to be reprimanded, Larisa advanced slowly across the room, conscious that the *Comte's* eyes were on her until she reached the desk.

She curtsied and waited for him to speak first.

"You are Miss Larisa Stanton?" he said, speaking to her surprise in almost perfect English.

"Yes, Monsieur le Comte."

"I have already learnt from my sister, Madame Savigny, that you appear to be a great deal younger than we had expected."

"I am sorry if I disappoint you, Monsieur le Comte."

"I did not say I was disappointed," the *Comte* said. "I was merely stating a fact. Governesses usually appear to be of an indeterminate age, but at least over thirty!"

There seemed to be no answer to this so Larisa remained silent.

After a moment the *Comte* said,

"You may sit down. I wish to talk to you."

"Thank you, *Monsieur.*"

Larisa sat herself on the edge of a hard-backed chair that was set in front of the desk.

She dropped her eyes conscious that the Comte was watching her.

"You are a good teacher?"

"I hope I may prove myself to be."

"This is your first situation?"

"Yes, *Monsieur*. I thought my Godmother, Lady Luddington, would have explained to the Comtesse de Chalon the reason why I am forced to seek employment.

"I was merely told," the *Comte* replied, "that you were a suitable person to enter my household and that your English would be impeccable."

"I hope that is true," Larisa answered. "My father, who wrote several books on Greek antiquities, was most particular that we should speak both eloquently and correctly."

"That is what I want for my grandson," the *Comte* said positively.

There was a pause before he went on,

"I can see now that I have met you, Miss Stanton, that you are different from what I expected, but it may be for the best."

Larisa's eyes were on his face as he continued,

"The women who have come here calling themselves governesses have had no idea how to teach. Jean-Pierre is an exceptional child. He is capable of learning only from someone who has gained his confidence."

"It is important, make no mistake about it from the very beginning, that he should be properly educated so that when the time comes he can take my place as the head of the family."

Larisa suppressed an inclination to say that that was obviously a long time ahead as the *Comte* continued,

"One day he will sit where I am sitting now. He will direct and rule over this estate, which has been in my family for over seven hundred years! He will add new laurels to our illustrious name and he will as a man be respected and admired."

It seemed to Larisa that the *Comte* spoke almost fanatically, and she understood what the nurse had meant when she said that Monsieur le Comte loved his grandson.

There was a pause in which Larisa felt she was expected to speak and after a moment she said softly,

"I will do what I can to make Jean-Pierre worthy of the ambitions you have for him, but at the moment he is only a child."

"The child becomes the man!" the *Comte* said. "You know the Jesuits say, 'Give me a child until he is seven and I will mould his character for life'!"

Larisa did not know what to reply to this, and then he said harshly,

"Let us hope that is not true. The fools, the imbeciles, who have tried to teach him up till now have gone the wrong way about it. They have antagonised him and turned him against learning. There is a shutter in a child's mind, which he can close when he does not wish to learn."

"I am sure that is true," Larisa said, "and I am sure it is no use absorbing a lot of facts until one understands what they mean."

"You are right there," the *Comte* agreed in a tone as if he were surprised at her observation.

"What I will try to do," Larisa said, "is to make Jean-Pierre interested in knowing more. That is the first step, I am sure, towards learning anything of value."

"You are obviously intelligent, Miss Stanton!" the *Comte* said. "At the same time Jean-Pierre is not an ordinary little boy. He is exceptional! And that is what I want him to be. Exceptional in every way! A credit to the house of Valmont!"

Again there was that strange, fanatical note in his voice before he continued,

"Can you imagine what it is like, Miss Stanton, to realise that the continuance of the family is centred in one child, one boy?

"To know that our history, which is a part of France, and a heritage that has inspired and sustained me all my life could end with my death?"

Larisa found herself longing to ask why everything should rest on Jean-Pierre. What about Comte Raoul? Surely he would inherit when the *Comte* died?

Comte Raoul was a young man. Why should he not marry again and have other children – another son?

Yet it seemed that Monsieur le Comte was ignoring his very existence.

It was of course impossible for her to put such ideas into words. All she could say was,

"I hope, *Monsieur*, that you will not expect results too quickly. First, I must get to know Jean-Pierre and he must get to know me. If he has been badly taught in the past it would be a mistake to worry him with lessons the moment we meet."

She thought for a moment then continued,

"I will talk to him first in his own language, then gradually hope to get him interested in learning English. In a house like this there must be fascinating history lessons in everything he sees."

The *Comte* seemed pleased at what she had said, although the severity of his face hardly relaxed.

"I will leave you to put your own methods into practice, Miss Stanton," he said, "but I wish to be kept informed of Jean-Pierre's progress. I do not want to be left in the dark. I will not be lied to. Do you understand? I will not listen to or hear any lies about him."

He spoke violently and for the first time since Larisa had been in the room he moved, bringing his fist down heavily on the desk in front of him so that the gold inkpot rattled.

"I can think of no reason why I should lie to you, *Monsieur*," Larisa said with dignity. "At the same time, I hope you will not frighten me."

"Frighten you?" Monsieur le Comte looked at her in surprise.

"I have told you quite honestly," Larisa said, "that this is the first time I have been a governess. I want to feel confident that I am doing the right thing and fear is very unsettling."

"I have a feeling, Miss Stanton," *le Comte* said, "that you are a somewhat unusual type of governess."

"My father disliked the whole race!" Larisa answered. "I am very anxious not to be one of the sort that he condemned as 'imbeciles'!"

"I think that is unlikely," *le Comte* replied.

For the first time Larisa thought there was an almost human expression on his face.

"That will be all, Miss Stanton," he said. "I shall see you and Jean-Pierre tomorrow when we meet at *déjeuner*. Unless there are guests, you bring him to the dining room."

"Thank you, *Monsieur*" Larisa said rising from her chair. She curtsied.

"Bonsoir, Mademoiselle" le Comte said in French.

"Bonsoir, Monsieur"

She moved towards the door.

Only when she was outside in the corridor did she realise she felt a little breathless, as if she had pitted herself against a blustery wind or a rough sea.

Le Comte was intimidating – there was no doubt about that!

The following morning Larisa was up early and was in the schoolroom before Nurse brought Jean-Pierre from the bedroom.

She did not know quite what she had expected.

Perhaps in her mind there had been a replica of the small boys with their dark hair and bright eyes she had seen running about the quayside when the steamer docked at Calais or in the crowds at the *Gare du Nord*, holding onto their parents' hands and getting in the way of porters, trucks and other passengers.

The little boy who came into the nursery was small for his age.

There was nothing sharp or dark about his features. He had large brown eyes and dark brown hair, and his complexion was fair. He had a small mouth that seemed to be perpetually smiling.

"Say 'how do you do' to *M'mselle*," Nurse admonished him.

Obediently he crossed the room and held out his hand to Larisa.

"How do you do, Jean-Pierre?" she said. "It is very nice to be here in your beautiful *Château* and I hope you are going to show me all the special things about it."

Jean-Pierre looked at her gravely for a moment and then he turned to Nurse with a smile.

"I want a little egg for breakfast – a little brown egg!"

"That is what you are going to have, my precious," Nurse answered.

As if she realised that Larisa would want an explanation she said,

"He has a fancy for bantam eggs and likes to go down to the farm to collect them himself."

"I am not surprised," Larisa replied. "I remember what fun it used to be when I was a child trying to find a new-laid egg."

"I want two brown eggs," Jean-Pierre insisted.

Two footmen appeared bringing in the breakfast. Larisa realised with an inward smile that while her supper could be handled by Suzanne, *le petit Monsieur* must be waited on with respect and grandeur.

The breakfast in fact was quite an elaborate meal, with the footmen handing the dishes and Jean-Pierre demanding what he wanted and, getting it, appeared to show little interest in anything else.

When they had finished and Suzanne had taken Jean-Pierre away to wash his hands, Larisa said to Nurse,

"I think it would be a good idea if we went out in the sunshine."

"No lessons?" Nurse asked.

"Not the sort one sits down at a desk to do," Larisa answered. "I want him to get to know, and if possible, to like me."

"You must give him time," Nurse said quickly.

"That is exactly what I intend to do," Larisa answered.

Jean-Pierre was quite ready to go for a walk.

He had very determined ideas of what he wished to do and was not very communicative when Larisa asked him questions.

He took her to the farm which was some way from the *Château*, and he chased the bantams to find out where they had laid their eggs in the hay and corn stacked in the farmyard.

Then he accepted a small basket of bantam eggs that had been kept ready for him to carry back to the *Château*.

As Larisa had anticipated, the *Château* in the daytime was overwhelmingly impressive.

It had been built early in the 18th century and it exemplified all the elegance, the beauty and the grandeur of the period.

Behind it were laid out formal gardens with their patterned flowerbeds, basins and fountains.

There was a vista cut through the forest that surrounded half the house to where, high on a hill in the distance, there was an elegant temple surrounded by stone statues.

Larisa could not help feeling how greatly her father would have appreciated them and although it was not his period, he would have admired the *Château* itself.

It was obvious that Jean-Pierre knew little about his home and Larisa made up her mind that she would find out the whole history of the *Château* and also of the Valmont family so that she could interest him in his inheritance.

As they walked around the gardens, she realised he was very young for his age.

He was also attracted by anything new that caught his attention, a butterfly or a bird would make him run after it with excitement, only in the next moment to be distracted by something else.

He however accepted her presence without comment and seemed to listen to what she said even while she was doubtful how much remained in his memory after she had finished speaking.

She told him stories about the flowers and tried to make him say their names in English, but he was more interested in the goldfish swimming in the fountain and after two or three English words made no effort to say any more.

'He must take his time,' Larisa told herself, 'I must not push him too hard. That is obviously what all the other governesses did.'

They walked back to the house in plenty of time for Jean-Pierre to tidy himself before he went down to luncheon with his grandfather.

It was hot and Larisa had chosen one of her cotton dresses in a shade of green, to which her mother had added a small white muslin collar and little white muslin cuffs.

She hoped it made her look demure. At the same time, she could not help noticing that the colour accentuated the gold of her hair and the clearness of her pink and white complexion.

'I doubt if anyone would notice it,' she told herself with a little grimace at her reflection in the mirror. 'I am sure Monsieur le Comte will have eyes only for his grandson.'

That was certainly true.

Larisa realised, as they sat in the huge Baronial dining room, waited on by the butler and several footmen, that *le Comte* ate very little and his eyes were constantly on his grandson's face.

"What did you do this morning, Jean-Pierre?" he asked.

There was a pause as if the small boy found it difficult to remember and then he said,

"Found lots of eggs – lots and lots!"

This was not true, but Larisa felt it wiser not to interrupt and after that *le Comte* enquired,

"And what else did you see?"

After a long pause Jean-Pierre replied,

"There were goldfish, little goldfish in the fountain."

Madame Savigny, who was sitting at the end of the table turned to Larisa.

"And what lessons did you do?" she asked.

"I tried to teach Jean-Pierre some of the English names, of the flowers," Larisa answered. "He pronounced them quite well."

She did not add that there were only three of them at which he had condescended to make an attempt.

She thought that *le Comte* looked at her briefly with approval.

"When Jean-Pierre has his rest after luncheon," Madame Savigny said, "I should be glad if you would come to my room, Miss Stanton. We had so little chance to talk last night on your arrival. There are so many things I would like you to tell me about yourself."

"Of course, *Madame*. That will be very pleasant," Larisa replied.

At the same time she could not help wondering if this was a new type of inquisition.

She was glad when luncheon ended.

There seemed to be an unnecessary number of courses and she was not surprised when Jean-Pierre, having eaten quite a large meal, became restless.

He fidgeted about on his chair and played with the knives and forks.

Larisa wondered if she ought to rebuke him but felt it was an uncomfortable thing to do in front of his grandfather.

Finally, Monsieur le Comte said,

"Jean-Pierre has finished. You can take him upstairs, Miss Stanton."

"Thank you, *Monsieur*."

Jean-Pierre would have jumped down from his chair but the *Comte* said sharply,

"Your Grace, Jean-Pierre, you have forgotten your Grace."

The small boy put his hands together in front of his face and gabbled a few words inaudibly.

Then he was running through the door and was halfway down the passage before Larisa could catch up with him.

The conversation with Madame Savigny was not as nerve-racking as she had expected.

In fact, the older woman unbent a little after Larisa had told her about her family and how her father had died leaving them no money, and that it was imperative that Nicky should finish his education at Oxford.

"How lucky you are to have so many sisters," Madame Savigny said.

"You have only one?" Larisa enquired.

Madame Savigny nodded.

"I never see her," she said. "She does not come home. She prefers Paris where she entertains a great deal."

"Paris is very exciting, I believe," Larisa said.

"Not for the *ancien régime*," Madame Savigny replied.

She saw that Larisa looked surprised and said,

"The last surviving descendants of Paris's illustrious Princely and Ducal families will not mix with the *bourgeoisie* who have risen in the world and who have no right to be representative of Society."

She spoke with a bitterness that astonished Larisa.

"The real Parisians," she said, "live in the *Faubourg St. Germain* and they dream of a restoration of the Royal Cause."

"They do not like the new Paris?" Larisa asked.

"They *hate* it!" Madame Savigny replied. "To them it is vulgar and *parvenu*, and so they do not mix but confine themselves to what is a world of their own."

She laughed rather scornfully as she added,

"Even electricity is too modern for them, and many noble householders continue to use oil lamps rather than the new lighting system about which there has been such a fuss."

"And things have not altered here, *Madame*?" Larisa ventured.

"My brother has seen to that," Madame Savigny replied. "No, nothing has altered and life at the Château Valmont is a trap from which none of us can escape."

She paused and added almost beneath her breath,

"Except Raoul – he got away."

Larisa looked at her in surprise. Then the older woman put her hand on her arm and said,

"You are young, *Mademoiselle*. Enjoy yourself while you can! Old age comes quickly and then there is nothing! Nothing to wait for but the grave!"

Larisa looked at her in bewilderment and Madame Savigny went on,

"Once I was young. Not as pretty as you, but still pretty enough, and I thought the world was a wonderful place where I would find happiness. But I was mistaken."

"You sound, *Madame,* as if you have been very unhappy?" Larisa said softly.

"Unhappy?" Madame Savigny repeated. "I can remember nothing but misery, ugliness and despair ever since I was twenty!"

"But why? *Why?"* Larisa asked.

"I should not be talking to you like this," Madame Savigny said. "It is just that you remind me of myself when I was young, so that I want to talk to you. There is no-one else here. They are all dead although they are still living. They are content with things as they are, but when I look back I see how different everything could have been."

"What happened?" Larisa asked almost beneath her breath.

She thought the older woman was going to refuse to answer her, but then she said in a low voice almost as if she spoke to herself,

"There was nothing I could do except to say goodbye to him. How could we run away together with no money? With nothing except our love for each other."

"Why did you have to say goodbye?" Larisa asked, almost afraid to ask the question in case she disrupted the revelations coming from the old lady's lips.

"My husband was a very rich man," Madame Savigny said simply. "The family were delighted when he asked for my hand in marriage. It was all arranged before I even saw him."

Larisa drew in her breath.

It was true then what her mother had said. This was what did happen in France.

"And the man you loved?" she asked.

"He also married a few years later, His wife is very rich. They live in the *Faubourg St. Germain* and she, entertains for him."

"I am sorry," Larisa said.

"Sometimes I used to think it would be better to be dead!" Madame Savigny went on. "My husband was soon bored with me, especially when I could not give him the children he required, and when he died he punished me in the same manner as he punished me during his lifetime by his neglect and indifference."

"What did he do?"

"He left all his money to his nephew to carry on his name. I had only a pittance and so I was forced to come back to Valmont. There was after that, no escape!"

There was so much unhappiness in the tired old voice that Larisa felt the tears come into her eyes.

"I am sorry ... *I am sorry,*" she said, but she knew as she spoke that sympathy was no consolation.

CHAPTER FOUR

"Une fleur pour Mademoiselle," Jean-Pierre said holding out a primrose he had picked in the wood.

"Thank you, Jean-Pierre!" Larisa replied, "but say it in English. Please say it in English."

He looked at her for a moment with his head on one side, then he said slowly,

"But-ter-fly,"

"No, no, Jean-Pierre. That is wrong," Larisa said. "Try again."

With a smile that she thought had a touch of mischief in it, Jean-Pierre said quickly,

"Good morn-ing! Good morn-ing!" and ran away between the trees.

Larisa gave a sigh that was half-frustration and half-despair.

She had been at the Château Valmont for two weeks and she had managed to teach Jean-Pierre exactly two words in English.

He applied the word 'butterfly' to anything that moved.

She had taught him 'good morning', and he had delighted his grandfather by saying it two days after she arrived.

But that was the net result of her labours and now, frighteningly, she had to face the truth that Jean-Pierre was not normal.

He was a lovable little boy who was no trouble to look after and who expressed his affection by bringing her little gifts.

Flowers, a stone, a stick! He brought them to her rather like a small puppy will retrieve any object that attracts him.

But when it came to lessons, she could neither coax nor command Jean-Pierre to learn anything.

She tried telling him stories, but after a few minutes his attention would wander, he would be distracted by something else and she would realise he was no longer listening.

She tried the most elementary arithmetic with bricks.

"One brick – two bricks, Jean-Pierre," she said speaking in French as she knew it was hopeless to make him understand English. "Say it after me, One . . . two."

"One . . . two . . ." Jean-Pierre would repeat obediently.

"And this is three," she would say putting down a third brick.

"One . . . two . . . one . . . two," Jean-Pierre would intone.

Larisa would lie awake at night wondering whether there was some special method by which she could reach him and hold his attention. Then she began to realise what the other governesses had found, that Jean-Pierre was unteachable.

At the back of her mind, although she tried not to think of it, was a boy who had lived in the village at Redmarley.

He had grown up strong and quite pleasant-looking and he had walked about the roads singing little songs to himself and being apparently quite happy.

They called him the village idiot, but everyone was kind to him and he appeared completely harmless.

Then one day, for no reason that anyone could ascertain, he strangled a child of three, after which he had been taken away and nobody heard of him again.

'Jean-Pierre could not be like that!' Larisa told herself.

Yet there was no escaping from the truth. Jean-Pierre had the mental abilities of a child of four or five.

She tried for a long time to tell herself she was imagining things but now every day that passed she realised sooner or later she had to come to a decision.

She must either tell Monsieur le Comte the truth, in which case he would undoubtedly dismiss her as he had dismissed other Governesses, or she could continue to pretend to teach Jean-Pierre knowing that her efforts were quite useless.

There was so much about the little boy that was attractive.

He had good manners. He was loving in the way of any engaging child. He would cuddle up beside her and put his head against her shoulder, he would kiss her goodnight because she told him to, and he was obedient when it suited him.

He seldom cried, and Larisa had never seen him angry or in a tantrum, which somehow seemed unnatural.

Nurse and Monsieur le Comte doted on him, but Larisa had the suspicion that Madame Savigny was more astute.

'What shall I do?' asked herself.

From her own point of view she was happy at the *Château*.

She never tired of looking at the beautiful painted and gilded rooms and the treasures that they contained, or of walking in the formal gardens seeing the fountains iridescent in the sunshine and the swans moving majestically in the moat.

It was like living in a fairy-tale and yet there were undercurrents and suppressed emotions that sometimes made her feel there were ugly and sinister shadows behind the sunlit exterior.

She had soon learnt from Nurse of the feud that existed between Monsieur le Comte and his son Comte Raoul.

"Why did they quarrel?" Larisa asked at last, although she knew the nurse might refuse to answer the question and she would be ashamed of being so curious.

"Monsieur le Comte insisted on Monsieur Raoul marrying when he was only twenty!" Nurse exclaimed. "His bride was chosen for him and he was not happy with the choice, but what could he do?"

She spread out her old hands expressively.

"Many times he said to me, 'I want to see a bit of the world before I settle down, *ma Bonne'*, which is what he calls me. 'I want to have some fun!'"

"I suppose it is what all young men want," Larisa said sympathetically.

"Monsieur le Comte would not listen," Nurse continued. "He forced Monsieur Raoul up the aisle, and of course from the point of view of the estate it was a good marriage."

She saw the question in Larisa's eyes and went on,

"The bride's dowry was 7,000 acres and a street in Paris."

"That must have pleased Monsieur le Comte!" Larisa exclaimed.

"Always he wants more and more for the estate," Nurse said. "Nothing matters but Valmont, which will one day belong to Jean-Pierre!"

"You were telling me about the quarrel,"

"Monsieur Raoul's wife died in childbirth," Nurse answered. "Almost before we were out of mourning

Monsieur le Comte was planning another marriage for Monsieur Raoul."

"Because he wanted more land?" Larisa asked.

"More children!" Nurse answered. "Can you not understand, *M'mselle?* Monsieur le Comte had only one son. After Monsieur Raoul was born the doctors said Madame la Comtesse could never have another child."

"So he wants grandchildren!"

"Many of them, to make sure of the inheritance. But Monsieur Raoul refused. They fought bitterly," Nurse said. "Finally, Monsieur le Comte threatened Monsieur Raoul that he would not give him one single Franc until he did as he was told."

"So what did he do?" Larisa asked.

"He defied his father and went to Paris."

Larisa was silent.

She wondered how Comte Raoul could give fantastic parties of the sort that Madame Madeleine had described to her if he had no money.

How had he survived? How had he managed to live after his father had refused to support him?

She had an idea, although she did not ask her, that Nurse would have no answer to this question.

What she said about Monsieur le Comte wanting grandchildren was confirmed in her conversation with Madame Savigny.

Not only had Nurse taken a fancy to Larisa, but Madame Savigny also talked to her as she had not been able to talk to anyone for years.

Sometimes Larisa thought the old woman forgot that she was not a contemporary as she poured out her troubles and chattered of family difficulties with a lack of reticence, which Larisa was certain was foreign to her natural reserve.

There was an explanation for this.

"I have been so very lonely, here these past years," she said to Larisa. "One cannot talk to servants and our neighbours have long since ceased to call."

"But why?" Larisa asked. "I thought that in France a great number of relatives often lived under the same roof."

"That is true," Madame Savigny agreed, "and when our father was alive the house was filled with people. There was our grandmother, several cousins, three old aunts, a Chaplain, a tutor for my brother and there were always friends and acquaintances staying with us and coming to meals."

"Then why does Monsieur le Comte not live in the same way?" Larisa asked.

"Because he will not spend the money," Madame Savigny replied. "He always says he cannot afford the expense of hospitality. We had some cousins living here for several years, but they were so unhappy they managed to scrape together enough to buy a small cottage in the Pyrenees."

"'Cousin Francois', they said to me before they left, "begrudges every crumb we put into our mouths. We cannot stand it any longer!'"

"Is Monsieur le Comte so hard-up?" Larisa asked.

She thought of the innumerable servants that filled the house, the great army of gardeners she had seen outside, the workers on the farm and in the woods.

"He says so," Madame Savigny answered, "and when I asked him the other day for a few francs with which to buy a new gown, he told me if I wanted one I should sell one of my rings!"

Everything, Larisa realised as her days passed on the Château Valmont, was destined for Jean-Pierre.

If Jean-Pierre wanted anything it was immediately forthcoming, and she began to think that the glories of the *Château* were kept up, not for Monsieur le Comte himself, but simply because Jean-Pierre's inheritance must be perfect.

One question trembled on her lips for a long time before finally she brought herself to ask Nurse,

"Does Monsieur Raoul ever come home?"

"Sometimes," Nurse replied, "and it is always a very happy day for me when I see my baby again, but he has not been here for over two years now and who shall blame him? Monsieur le Comte made it very clear that he was not welcome."

"Yet one day he will inherit all this. Surely it must come to him before it goes to Jean-Pierre?" Larisa asked.

"Of course," Nurse answered, "but Monsieur le Comte always speaks as if he had no son. He tries to obliterate Monsieur Raoul from his thoughts."

It was sad, Larisa thought, that in such a beautiful *Château* and in such exquisite surroundings people could not be happy.

She wondered how she could ever tell Monsieur le Comte the truth about Jean-Pierre.

She had the feeling that it would destroy him when finally he realised that his only grandson would never be capable of taking his place at the head of the family.

'I must try! I must try harder to get through to Jean-Pierre,' Larisa thought desperately. 'There must be something I can do!'

She realised that, while she had been thinking, Jean-Pierre, zig-zagging about in between the trees was some distance away from her.

Picking up her skirts she started to run down the mossy path.

"Jean-Pierre!" she called, "wait for me!"

He glanced around and seeing she was running after him smiled mischievously.

"Catch me, *Mademoiselle*! Catch me!" he called.

Then he tore off at such a speed that Larisa was afraid he would vanish from her sight. All she could do was to run faster in an effort to catch up with him.

Gradually the gap between them closed and she had almost reached him when running through the trees she came upon the wide grass ride that divided two woods from one another.

Jean-Pierre rushed across it, still intent on evading her, then as Larisa followed him she saw that he had run right in front of a horse and rider.

The sudden appearance of the child frightened the horse – a big black stallion – and he reared up in the air.

His rider pulled him back almost to his haunches and with an almost superhuman effort Larisa, darting forward, managed to catch hold of Jean-Pierre and drag him to safety from right under the horse's hoofs.

Breathless, both with the speed at which she had run and the fear that Jean-Pierre would be hurt, she held him close against her, her blue eyes wide with anxiety as the rider got his frightened horse under control.,

Then he turned towards Larisa and said furiously,

"What in God's name do you mean by letting the child run out like that? He might have been knocked down and killed!"

For a moment Larisa could not find her voice to answer the accusation. Then as she looked up into the rider's face she knew who spoke.

Never had she imagined that a man could look so dashing, so smart, and at the same time have the appearance of what she could only describe to herself as the devil!

It was Comte Raoul – there was no doubt about that!

Who else, she thought, could look as he did and simultaneously, despite his anger and the frown between his eyes, seem almost irresistibly attractive?

He was not as handsome as Nicky. No-one would ever have mistaken him for a god, Greek or otherwise.

But something in the angle of his high hat, the carnation in his buttonhole, and the way he sat on the big black stallion made Larisa feel that he had come straight out of a fairy story.

He was undoubtedly part of the whole strange, enchanting, unpredictable allure of the Château Valmont.

As she did not reply Comte Raoul swung himself down from the saddle and, patting his horse's neck, said,

"I might have guessed it would be you, Jean-Pierre! Surely you know by this time that you should not be running about on 'the gallop'?" But Jean-Pierre was not attending to him.

"Horse!" he said with pleasure. "Nice horse!"

He moved forward without fear and Comte Raoul made his horse lower his head so that Jean-Pierre could pat his nose.

Then he looked at Larisa and said,

"I think we should introduce ourselves. I am Raoul de Valmont."

"I am Jean-Pierre's new English governess, *Monsieur.*"

As Larisa spoke she was conscious that having run so swiftly after Jean-Pierre the little straw hat that she had been wearing had blown from her head and was hanging down her back suspended by the ribbons that had been tied under her chin.

The sunshine was therefore on her fair hair and the eyes that she raised to Comte Raoul's face were very blue.

"Governess!" he exclaimed. "And where can my father have found anyone so unique? You are, *Mademoiselle,* not in the least like your predecessors!"

"So I understand," Larisa answered demurely.

"You must tell me how Jean-Pierre is getting on with his lessons. As you know I have a proprietory interest in him."

"Yes, Monsieur."

"Have you been here long?"

"Two weeks, *Monsieur.*"

"So long?" he asked with mock gravity, "and you have found the dust of ages too stifling during that period?

"I think the *Château* is the most beautiful place I have ever seen, *Monsieur.*"

"And the people in it?" he enquired.

She realised as he spoke that one of the most attractive things about him, and at the same time the most disconcerting, was the way that his eyes, dark and twinkling, seemed to say far more than his lips.

She had not realised that a man could have such a vivid face or such an expressive one.

Because she felt shy of the look in his eyes, she dropped her own and busied herself by untying the ribbons around her neck.

Jean-Pierre was already bored with patting the horse and was running about on the grass.

"Would you like a ride, Jean-Pierre?" Comte Raoul enquired.

The child's eyes lit up.

"Ride?" he questioned.

Comte Raoul lifted him up in his arms and set him in the saddle.

"Has he started riding yet?" he asked Larisa.

"Not since I have been here, *Monsieur*."

"I expect my father is afraid that he will break his neck!" Comte Raoul said sarcastically. "If the child is never allowed to take part in any sport in case he damages himself, he will grow up to be a complete moron."

That, Larisa thought, was what he might be anyway, but she answered quietly,

"Jean-Pierre is fond of animals. Perhaps I could suggest to Monsieur le Comte that he has a pony."

"I should do that! Since he is as you say fond of animals I have brought him a present, which I am sure he will like."

Jean-Pierre was holding onto the saddle, apparently quite happy to be on the big stallion. Comte Raoul took the bridle and they walked forward down the ride towards the *Château*, which they could see in the distance.

"What is his present?" Larisa enquired. "Or is it a secret, Monsieur?"

"It should be at the *Château* by the time we get there," Comte Raoul answered. "My groom has it, with him in my phaeton, which also contains my luggage."

"You have come to stay?"

She felt even as she uttered the words that they perhaps sounded impertinent, but they were said before she could prevent them.

"You sound surprised!" Comte Raoul said accusingly.

"I am sure it will also surprise my father. I have things which I wish to discuss with him."

"Yes, yes of course," Larisa said, feeling embarrassed that she had been so forward.

"It is obviously time I returned home," Comte Raoul went on. "I never expected there would be such a notable addition to the family since I was last here – or such an attractive one!"

There was no mistaking his meaning and Larisa felt the flush rise in her cheeks. This she told herself, was just the sort of compliment her mother had warned her about.

She looked ahead to where at the end of the ride she could now see the Cupola, which surmounted the centre of the *Château*.

She was aware that Comte Raoul's eyes were on her profile and after a moment he said,

"You are lovely! Quite incredibly lovely! But a lot of men must have told you that."

"No they have not!" Larisa said firmly, "because *Monsieur*, they had better manners!"

~93~

She meant to be reproving, but she saw Comte Raoul smile and the flash of his eyes as he said,

"Is it bad-mannered to tell the truth? I should have thought you of all people, would have appreciated frankness and honesty."

"My nurse always said," Larisa answered, "that personalities are odious!"

"I am quite certain my nurse said the same thing!" Comte Raoul retorted. "But you can hardly expect me not to be surprised at your appearance and the fact that you can find nothing better to do with it than bury yourself in what to all intents and purposes is a cemetery!"

"I am very happy at the *Château, Monsieur*," Larisa said. "And now if you will lift Jean-Pierre down from your horse, I think we should hurry back. It will soon be time for luncheon."

"I am taking you back," Comte Raoul replied. "I doubt if you have as yet discovered all the short-cuts. I can get you there far quicker than you can manage."

There was nothing Larisa could do.

She lifted her chin a little higher and she walked quicker so that he would be obliged in his turn to quicken his pace.

"I have always been told," he said after a moment, "that English women are very strait-laced. At the same time as you have to earn your own living, you cannot be as young or as unsophisticated as you appear. Did you travel to France alone?"

"I had no difficulty in doing so, *Monsieur.*"

"No romantic encounters? Or perhaps you enjoy them? I am sure there were dozens of gentlemen only too willing to assist you with your baggage."

"There were only porters, *Monsieur*, concerned wholly with how large a *pourboire* I intended to give them."

"You are very prosaic," the Comte said accusingly. "Was it not in fact something of an adventure?"

Larisa repressed an inclination to agree that in fact, that was what it had been.

She must not encourage him, she thought.

He was too obviously at his ease, too certain that she would be amused and interested by everything he had to say.

Yet at the same time she could not help being tinglingly conscious of his walking beside her.

"Le Diable", Madame Madeleine had said he was called, and she had no intention of letting him tempt her into any sort of indiscretion.

"Tell me about yourself," he asked beguilingly.

"You would not be interested, *Monsieur*"

"But I am – *very* interested. The more I look at you the more I am spellbound and incredibly curious as to why you have come to Valmont."

"I wanted a post as a governess."

"But why? There must have been so many other possibilities.'"

He spoke so positively that Larisa could not help telling the truth.

"Actually, there were none!"

"I do not believe it! Are all the men in England blind? Or have you perhaps stepped down from Olympus to bemuse and bewilder mere humans, who see you as someone they have dreamt of but never thought would materialise?"

His reference to Olympus made Larisa want to laugh.

None of the Stantons, she thought, could get away from the Greek image that had been their father's perception of what they should look like.

"Why are you smiling?" the *Comte* asked quickly.

"A family joke, *Monsieur*. You would not understand."

He thought for a moment and then he said,

"Was it because I referred to you as coming from Olympus? You look like a Greek goddess, and do not tell me that you are unaware of it. You are far too intelligent!"

The only answer to that, Larisa thought, was silence and she walked on without speaking until he said,

"What is your name?"

"Stanton," she said, "Larisa Stanton."

"So I was right!" he exclaimed. "I have been to Larisa. It is in a lovely part of Greece."

"That is what my father thought."

"So he Christened you after it?"

"Yes, *Monsieur*."

"Well, tell me more. Why was your father in Greece, and why . . . ?"

He stopped.

"Mon Dieu!" he exclaimed, "you are being very difficult! Can it be that my reputation has preceded me even to the Château Valmont?"

He spoke with such a mocking note in his voice that Larisa could not help smiling even while she tried to prevent herself from doing so.

"You should know," Comte Raoul said sternly, "that governesses must never listen to gossip. They should trust their instincts, their senses and their eyes."

"Perhaps that is what I am doing, *Monsieur!*"

"Now you are definitely being unkind," he protested. "I am not certain that you are the right person to teach Jean-Pierre. A child should learn only what is beautiful. Ugliness comes all too quickly once we have grown up."

Larisa thought there was a bitter note in the Comte's voice, but she merely said,

"That is what I would like to teach him, but even when we are old we can avoid the ugly things if we are sensible."

"Do you really believe that?" Comte Raoul asked and now there was no doubt that he was being cynical.

"Yes, I do believe it," Larisa answered. "It is our own fault if we give in, if we let other people spoil all that is finest and best in ourselves, so that we become embittered."

She was thinking as she spoke how they all as a family had faced the difficulties that came to light after her father's death.

They had been concerned, upset and unhappy, but they had not been bitter or cynical about it.

"You speak as if you had just surmounted a personal problem and found that it did not affect you intrinsically."

Larisa decided he was much more perceptive than she had imagined he would be.

"That is true," she said, "but perhaps my problem was not as difficult as it might have been because it was shared."

"With a man?" Comte Raoul asked sharply.

"No, with my family."

"Then you are fortunate. My family is prepared to share nothing with me."

There was no mistaking now, the cynicism in his tones and Larisa said without thinking,

"It takes two to make a quarrel."

"In which case you cannot know my father."

"I dare say he is very difficult," Larisa conceded, "everyone has told me so. At the same time, he has two great loves in his life – Valmont and Jean-Pierre."

"And one great hatred," Comte Raoul added. "Me!"

There seemed to be no answer to that, and as Larisa did not speak he said after a moment,

"Well? What is your magic to cure or prevent such animosity? Surely a goddess has some solution?"

"I think you should try to find one," Larisa said, "both for his sake and for yours."

As she spoke she thought what a strange conversation this was to hold with a man she had only just met! The man whom she had been warned against and who was to many people the personification of wickedness.

Yet strangely she found herself feeling sorry for him.

He might have all Paris at his feet, but this was his home and she knew, without Comte Raoul telling her so, that he anticipated that his arrival would not be welcomed and that he would be received with hostility.

They were almost at the *Château*, and as they reached the bridge across the moat Larisa saw standing at the front door a very smart phaeton drawn by two magnificent horses.

The coachman was in the yellow and black livery worn by the retainers of Monsieur le Comte, but it was far smarter and cut in a different style.

There was another man in front of the phaeton who Larisa guessed from his appearance to be a valet.

She knew she was not mistaken when as they approached them the man jumped to the ground and lifted down a small brown and white spaniel.

"There is your present, Jean-Pierre," Comte Raoul said to the small boy on his horse.

"A dog!" Jean-Pierre exclaimed, "a little dog!"

He was in such a hurry to get down from the stallion that Comte Raoul only just caught him as he tried to jump down by himself.

He put him on the ground and Jean-Pierre ran forward to where the valet stood holding the dog by a lead.

"A dog! *A dog!*" Jean-Pierre cried and put his arms around the animal's neck without a touch of fear.

"He is fond of animals," Larisa said, "it was kind of you to buy it for him."

Comte Raoul looked at her with a smile.

"I will be honest Miss Stanton, and tell you that the dog was a present to myself, which I found somewhat embarrassing, and I could think of no better way to dispose of it except to bring it to Valmont."

"It will certainly make Jean-Pierre very happy if he is allowed to keep it," Larisa said. Even as she expressed the doubt she knew that if Jean-Pierre was determined to have the dog his grandfather would agree.

She moved towards the little boy and bent down to stroke the dog's head.

"Un chien, Mademoiselle, un petit chien!" Jean-Pierre said with an ecstatic expression on his face.

"I think we had better take him up to the schoolroom and show him to Nurse," Larisa suggested. "Will you thank your father for the present and ask him what is the dog's name?"

"I have so far not Christened it," Comte Raoul said, "but as he was given to me at *Maxim's*, I imagine that 'Max' would be an appropriate and easy name to remember."

Larisa had the feeling that he was deliberately trying to make her curious as to who should have given him a dog at *Maxim's*.

But she did not raise her eyes to his face as she took Jean-Pierre by the hand and said again,

"Thank your father. Thank him very much."

"Merci! Merci!" Jean-Pierre said automatically.

Why not say it in English?" the *Comte* suggested. Because she felt it was expected of her Larisa said, "Say thank you in English, Jean-Pierre."

"Good morning!" Jean-Pierre replied.

Then pulling the dog by the lead he ran up the steps and into the house.

"A great achievement, Miss Stanton!" Comte Raoul remarked.

She knew that his eyes were twinkling and he was deliberately trying to provoke her.

Larisa half expected that as Comte Raoul was there for luncheon, she and Jean-Pierre would eat in the schoolroom.

But when she told Nurse that Comte Raoul had arrived the old woman became extremely excited, and insisted that they should both go downstairs to luncheon.

"If Monsieur le Comte does not want you, he will say so, she said. In any case I think it is better you should be there."

"Better?" Larisa queried even while she knew the answer.

She found Monsieur le Comte and Madame Savigny in the salon with Comte Raoul.

She thought that Monsieur le Comte was looking particularly aloof and disdainful until he saw his grandson. Then his eyes softened and he held out his hand as Jean-Pierre ran across the room to him.

"Dog! *I have a dog!*" the little boy cried.

"So I have heard," Monsieur le Comte replied.

His lips tightened as he added,

"Your father knows very well I have never allowed dogs in the *Château* – they are destructive!"

"I am sure we can keep Max in the schoolroom," Larisa said quietly.

Monsieur le Comte gave her a look as if her intervention was quite uncalled for. Then before he could reply luncheon was announced.

They sat down in the big Baronial dining hall and Jean-Pierre was as usual too intent upon his food to take much notice of anything else.

Larisa could feel the tension between father and son although Comte Raoul seemed at his ease, and there was no doubt that Madame Savigny was pleased to have him there.

"It is too long since we have seen you, Raoul," she said. "Here at Valmont we might be a million miles away from

Paris. No-one tells us what is going on. Are you enjoying yourself?"

"But of course," Comte Raoul replied. "Paris, Aunt Emilie is full of joy. There are a great many visitors to our city and they all want to be entertained in the typical Parisian manner."

"And that, I suppose," Monsieur le Comte remarked, "means spending money."

"Naturally, Father," Comte Raoul answered, "the theatres, the restaurants, the *cafés chantants*, and of course the *Folies Bergères*, are all expensive!"

Larisa saw the expression of disgust that crossed the face of Monsieur le Comte, and she realised that Comte Raoul had seen it too because he said quickly in a very different tone,

"But I am not here to talk about Paris, Father, which I know always annoys you, or indeed to distress you with my extravagances, but to tell you how you can make money."

"Make money?" Monsieur le Comte spluttered.

"Yes, indeed – and it is a proposal that I think will interest you."

There was a serious expression on his face. Larisa had the idea that he had opened the subject while they were at the luncheon table because in that way he could force his father to listen to him.

She felt that what he was about to say was of tremendous importance and he needed the support of his aunt.

"What is it? What are you talking about?" Monsieur le Comte enquired.

"We have grown wine here on our estate for generations," Comte Raoul replied. "Many years ago we grew a little champagne, but for the last fifty years at any rate we have concentrated on our ordinary wine."

"Which is good – exceptionally good!" Monsieur le Comte said aggressively.

"I agree with you, Father, but as you must know every year champagne is becoming more and more popular. I have at the moment the opportunity of buying a vineyard."

He paused, his eyes on his father's face.

"It is near Epernay, in what is known as the Champagne Country, and has in the past produced an excellent quality champagne. But it has been mismanaged, the owner has died, and his family no longer wish to carry on. I have for one week, the first refusal of 500 acres!"

There was silence for a moment and then Monsieur le Comte said,

"Am I supposed to guess what you intend to do about it?"

"I am suggesting that *we* should do something about it, Father. It is, I believe, a splendid investment and we should get big returns almost immediately on our money. Because my friends wish to do me a favour, we can buy the vineyard for a very reasonable sum and this year's harvest alone should pay back a great deal of the original expenditure."

Monsieur le Comte did not speak and after a moment Comte Raoul went on,

"I have brought with me plans, reports and an expert's estimation of the potential of the vineyard for the next five years."

Still Monsieur le-Comte did not reply and his face seemed expressionless.

Comte Raoul continued,

"The worldwide demand for champagne from France increases. Last year nearly twenty-five million bottles were sold. Yet only 20% of what is bottled is exported. Great Britain is France's biggest customer, followed by Russia!"

"And who drinks it?" Monsieur le Comte asked speaking for the first time. "Fools and wasters like yourself! Evil livers, spendthrifts, gamblers! Wine is good enough for the true Frenchman like myself. I shall continue to drink what my grandfather and his grandfather before him drank."

"You can drink what you like," Comte Raoul said, "but why not improve the family exchequer, which you always tell me is impoverished? You have the chance to own a vineyard in the very heart of the champagne district, knowing that you can sell every bottle before the crops are even picked?"

"No!"

The monosyllable rang out in the dining room and now Monsieur le Comte's face was no longer expressionless.

"Do you think I would listen to any of your wildcat schemes?" he asked. "Do you think I would sink to associate with the type of people that you call your friends? Do you think I would trust you with the Valmont money, which I have kept from running through your fingers and from being thrown away in the gutters of Paris?"

As he spoke Monsieur le Comte pushed back his chair.

"There is no more to be said on the matter," he remarked and now his voice was cold and icy.

He was turning towards the door when Comte Raoul spoke again.

"In which case, Father, I shall buy the vineyard myself!"

It seemed that his words arrested Monsieur le Comte. His eyes met his son's and he asked as if he could not help himself,

"And how will you manage to do that?"

"I shall borrow the money, Father, on the prospect of my inheritance. That at least you cannot keep me from having!"

An expression of anger contorted Monsieur le Comte's face.

For a moment Larisa thought he would either lash out with his tongue at Comte Raoul or even step forward to strike him.

Then with what was a tremendous effort at self-control he turned and walked from the dining room.

Later, when Larisa had taken Jean-Pierre up to the schoolroom for his rest, she went as usual to Madame Savigny's sitting room.

It had become a habit for her to have an hour's talk with the old lady while Jean-Pierre slept, and she found, as she expected, Madame Savigny was waiting for her.

She was sitting in her usual chair, and as Larisa entered the room she was wiping her eyes with a small muslin handkerchief.

"You must not be upset, *Madame*," Larisa said sympathetically.

"It is always the same," Madame Savigny said helplessly. "Whenever Raoul comes home – and I do so long to see him – he upsets his father and they have these terrible fights, which make me so unhappy."

"Try not to disturb yourself," Larisa begged.

She sat down beside Madame Savigny.

"It is foolish of me to cry," the latter said, "but I hate angry voices and cross words. My brother has always been the same if anyone disagrees with him."

"It is fortunate we are not living in ancient times when, if he were a King, he would say 'off with his head!'"

Madame Savigny smiled as Larisa had intended her to do.

"You are right!" she said. "That is exactly what he would say to poor Raoul."

"Who is talking about me?" a voice asked from the doorway, and Comte Raoul came into the sitting room.

"You two look as if you are intriguing," he said as he crossed the room.

He had changed from his riding clothes for luncheon, and Larisa thought it would be impossible for any man to be more elegant or more dashing.

It was not the clothes themselves. There was nothing flashy about them. It was just the air with which he wore them, and he himself was so unexpressively vital that everything he touched seemed to vibrate with him.

Larisa rose to her feet.

"I will leave you," she said quietly to Madame Savigny.

"Oh no, dear! Do not go," Madame Savigny begged.

"If you leave on my account, Miss Stanton," Comte Raoul said, "I shall feel guilty."

"I thought perhaps you would wish to speak with your aunt alone," Larisa explained.

"What I have to say can be listened to by both of you."

Comte Raoul sat down in a chair and bent towards his aunt.

"Have you no influence with Father, Aunt Emilie? This is a really tremendous opportunity and actually I brought

~106~

the idea to him as a kind of peace offering. He always cries poverty, and the vineyard, I know, will make a really large amount of money."

"If *you* had not suggested it, Raoul, perhaps he would have considered it," Madame Savigny replied. "But you know what he is like where you are concerned."

"As I have not seen him for so long, I had forgotten how virulent he could be," Comte Raoul sighed. "It does not seem possible in this day and age that a mediaeval feud could go on between father and son for ever."

"Your father has always been the same," Madame Savigny said.

"Which is no consolation at the moment," Comte Raoul remarked. "I want that vineyard and I intend to have it!"

"But how?" Madame Savigny asked.

"I shall find the money, I shall beg, borrow or steal it, as I have had to do in the past."

"You are quite certain it will be a success?" Larisa asked.

"I know a lot about champagne," Comte Raoul answered, "and not only because I drink it!"

"When was the making of champagne first discovered?" Larisa asked.

"The champagne vine known as *Vitis Vinifera* has been cultivated in Europe since the days of the Phoenicians," Comte Raoul replied.

He added with a smile,

"Has nobody told you that the wine that is so intrinsically connected with frivolity, gaiety and beautiful women owes its existence to a monk?"

"To a monk?" Larisa exclaimed in surprise.

"He was a Benedictine called Dom Perignon who in 1668 was appointed Chief Cellarer of a monastery on the Mountain of Rheims called *Hautvillas*."

"How fascinating!"

"It occurred to him," Comte Raoul continued, "that it might be possible to develop the natural sparkle in the wine and he embarked on experiments which lasted for twenty years."

"And he succeeded?"

"In 1690 he achieved his ambition of producing a bottle of truly sparkling champagne."

"Many people must have been grateful to him."

"They were! Champagne was introduced in the fast, extravagant, improper reign of the Regent, Phillippe Duc d'Orleans! The orgies of the Palais Royal were as notorious as my own!"

Comte Raoul smiled, disarmingly and went on,

"At a party near Paris given in 1716 by the Duc de Vendome, twelve luscious girls scantily dressed as Bacchautes presented every-guest with a pear-shaped bottle of champagne!"

"And they liked it?" Larisa asked.

"By the end of supper, the success of sparkling champagne in France was assured! The Abbé de Chaulieu wrote,

'Hardly was it served, than from my mouth it passed into my heart!'"

Larisa clapped her hands.

"What a tribute!"

"It not only warmed their breasts!" Comte Raoul said, "it filled their pockets."

"If I had any money of my own, I would help you buy your vineyard, Raoul," Madame Savigny said.

"I know you would, Aunt Emilie, you have always supported me and found excuses for me even when I was at my worst!"

"I never believed all the things they said about you," Madame Savigny said gently.

"You can believe most of them!" Comte Raoul replied. "At the same time, I am now getting older. I want an interest apart from the frothy frivolities of Paris. I hoped, it was stupid of me I know, that Father would buy the vineyard and let me run it for him."

"And now?"

"I will buy it myself. I shall buy it, but it will not be as easy as it might have been! And it will not at the moment, as I had hoped, become part of the Valmont Estate."

There was a moment's pause before Madame Savigny said in a quavering voice,

"You still – care for Valmont?"

"Care for it?" Comte Raoul asked. "It is mine and a part of me. Make no mistake, Aunt Emilie. Whatever Father may say, one day I shall live here. One day I shall be able once again to think of it as home."

CHAPTER FIVE

Larisa walked into the schoolroom having changed for dinner.

She found Nurse there and the two women looked at each other in an understanding manner.

"They have been talking together all afternoon," Nurse said in a low voice and there was no mistaking of whom she spoke.

There was a question in Larisa's eyes and Nurse continued,

"I think the situation has improved a little. Bernard told me just now that Monsieur Raoul asked his father for a case of the Valmont wine and Monsieur le Comte said he could have one of the 1874 vintage which is kept for very special occasions."

Larisa knew that Bernard was Monsieur le Comte's manservant who was closely in his confidence.

Everything that went on in the *Château* was relayed to its owner by Bernard, and if he thought things were going better than they had done before, then there must indeed be an improvement.

"I hope you are right," Larisa said.

She wondered as she spoke whether Monsieur le Comte would in fact give in and agree to purchase the vineyard.

It seemed somehow unlikely in view of the manner in which he had behaved at luncheon.

At the same time she was certain that Comte Raoul could be very persuasive.

"If only we could all live in peace," Nurse said almost beneath her breath. Then as she wiped her eyes she added,

"When Monsieur Raoul came to see me today he said, 'I wish I was young again, *ma Bonne*, the same age as Jean-Pierre, and have you making all the decisions for me. How easy it would be!'"

As if the memory of what Comte Raoul had said was too much for her, Nurse went from the schoolroom and Larisa knew it was to hide her tears.

Larisa ate little of the delicious dishes that the chef had sent up for her supper.

She did not feel hungry and felt somehow emotionally involved in the drama that was taking place in the household.

Even though she told herself it was none of her business and she was outside everything that happened, she could not help feeling concerned.

There was also at the back of her mind, although she tried not to think of it, the knowledge that sooner or later Monsieur le Comte would have to know about Jean-Pierre.

It opened up the question as to whether it would make him kinder or more vehement against his only son.

When Larisa had finished her supper and Suzanne had taken away the tray, she picked up a book intending to read. But she found it impossible to concentrate and she must have sat for a long time deep in her thoughts, the book open on her lap.

Then came a knock at the door.

"Entrez!"

A footman stood there.

"Monsieur wishes to speak to you in the Blue Cabinet, *M'mselle.*"

"I will come downstairs in a moment," Larisa answered.

She went to her bedroom to see that her hair was tidy and to pick up a handkerchief.

She was wearing a thin muslin gown she had made herself, which had a pattern of small, blue flowers on it and a sash of the same colour that matched her eyes.

She took a quick glance at her reflection in a long mirror and then went down the stairs.

She was surprised that Monsieur le Comte had not asked her to come to the salon where he habitually sat.

Then as she neared the Blue Cabinet, which was a small room exquisitely decorated in blue and gold to match the *Sèvres* china arranged on inlaid enamelled tables, she realised that the footman had not said it was 'Monsieur le Comte' who wished to see her.

She therefore half-expected that Comte Raoul would be waiting. As she entered the small room a man turned from the window and she saw that she had not been mistaken.

She stood still just inside the door and did not realise how very young, lovely and vulnerable she looked.

Her fair hair was silhouetted against the blue of the walls and when her eyes turned to his, they were a little apprehensive with perhaps a shadow of fear in them.

For a moment Comte Raoul stood looking at her without speaking, and then he said,

"I want to talk to you. Shall we go outside? It is a warm evening."

There was a serious tone in his voice, which Larisa had not expected and she acquiesced without replying, moving across the room as he opened the long window a little wider so that they could both step out onto the terrace.

There was a small footbridge spanning the moat on this side of the *Château* and they crossed over it onto a green lawn and proceeded down a path which took them up the side of the formal garden.

They walked in the shadow of the trees moving away from the house and were climbing, Larisa realised, towards the Grecian Temple, which stood at the end of the long vista beyond the fountains.

She had a strange feeling as she moved beside the Comte that there was no need for words.

It was as if they were talking to each other, and yet he had not spoken since they left the *Château*.

Finally, they came to where below the Temple there was a white statue set against a high yew-hedge and in front of it a seat.

Comte Raoul stopped, made a gesture with his hand and Larisa sat down.

As he seated himself beside her she realised that they looked down at the *Château* and in the diffusion of golden light of the sun, which had just set below the horizon, it looked like an exquisite jewel.

With its perfect symmetry, its cupola, its stone carvings and iridescent windows reflected in the moat, it was difficult to imagine that it was real and not part of a dream. Still Comte Raoul did not speak but sat looking at the *Château* until at last Larisa said hesitatingly,

"Why do you not do as your father . . . wishes?"

"Marry again?"

"Charles II said 'England was worth a Mass'. Is not Valmont worth a marriage?"

"Not of his choosing! No – never, never again!"

He spoke violently and Larisa realised that his marriage had not only been disastrous but the hurt of it still remained.

"I am . . . sorry," she murmured.

"For me? I do not want your pity!"

"Not only for you, but for Valmont,' Larisa said. "It is so beautiful! I feel that it is a house made for happiness, if only one could find the right formula for it."

There was silence for a moment and then Comte Raoul said,

"I am frightened!"

"Frightened?" Larisa asked, "but why?"

"Something strange and incredible has happened," he replied, "something I never expected. I cannot for the moment quite believe it."

Larisa thought he would go on, but after a pause she asked, tentatively,

"Will you tell me what is . . . frightening you?"

"When we met this morning," he answered, "and I swore at you because Jean-Pierre startled my horse, what did you think of me?"

Larisa's lips parted in a little smile.

"I thought that you looked . . . exactly as I had expected you to do."

"You knew who I was?"

"Yes, of course. No-one else could look quite like that!"

"Like what?"

She realised it would be embarrassing to answer that question. She had thought how dashing and smart he had appeared.

At the same time, he did have the appearance of a devil!

She did not reply and after a moment he said,

"I can imagine how I appeared. At the same time you recognised me?"

"Yes."

"Just as I recognised you."

Larisa turned to look at him in perplexity.

"How can you have done that?" she asked. "You had never heard of me. You had no idea I would be here."

"Nevertheless, I recognised you," he insisted, "because I had always known that somewhere in the world there would be someone who looked like you!"

"I do not think I . . . understand, *Monsieur.*"

"I do not understand it myself," Comte Raoul replied, "and therefore it is almost impossible for me to put into words, but I have always known that you existed somewhere, and when I saw you, you were exactly as I expected you to be!"

Larisa looked at him in astonishment, and now he turned his head to look into her eyes.

"When I looked down at you with your arms around Jean-Pierre I knew I had found what I had always been seeking."

There was an expression in his eyes that held her spellbound and she was unable to move.

"Not quite consciously perhaps," he went on in a low voice, "but I was continually disappointed, disillusioned, always wanting something I could not express. *It was you!*"

It was hard to breathe until with an effort she turned her eyes from his to look at the house below them.

"I think," she said, and her voice was uncertain, "that you are only imagining what you say you feel."

"That is what I have tried to tell myself," he replied, "but it is not true."

There was a little silence and then he said,

"Perhaps we have met before in a previous life. Perhaps you have occupied secretly a special shrine in my heart. I do not know. I do not understand. I am waiting for you to explain it to me."

Larisa remembered how she had spoken to Nicky of reincarnation and yet now she was faced with the idea it seemed impossible. Just a theory that could never be substantiated.

"I have . . . no explanation," she said after a moment.

"What had you been told about me?" he asked.

"I met a woman on the train," Larisa replied, "a dressmaker called Madame Madeleine, who told me of your . . . parties."

"And she warned you against me?"

"Y-yes."

"I can guess what she said, but now when you see me in my own home what do you think of me?"

"I am . . . sorry for you. At the same time perhaps your father has good reason to dislike the life you lead."

"He has every reason, but he forced it upon me," Comte Raoul said, and there was a bitterness in his voice. "You do not understand that I had no choice except to obey him blindly."

Larisa remembered what Nurse had told her about Comte Raoul being forced up the aisle when he was twenty, when he had no wish to marry.

Because she wanted to make things better, to help the man sitting beside her she said softly,

"Could you not persuade your father to let bygones be bygones and start again? The quarrel does not hurt only you. It hurts everyone who lives at Valmont."

"I know that," the Comte said, "and they are my people. Mine because most of the employees on the estate have lived here for generations. They are as much a part of the family as those who actually have Valmont blood running in their veins."

"I can understand your thinking like that," Larisa said.

"But all the time my father is cheese-paring where he could expand," Comte Raoul went on. "I visited our vineyards and farms a little while ago, without his being aware of it, and he is using old-fashioned methods. He will not buy new machinery. He has uneconomical methods of storage. The whole estate could be improved. We need new houses, more workers."

He spoke vehemently. Then his voice died away.

"What is the point of even talking about it?" he asked.

"The old man will not listen to me."

"Nurse thought things were perhaps going better this evening," Larisa said. "I was told Monsieur le Comte had given you a case of his best wine."

"I asked him for a case," Comte Raoul said, "not only because I thought it would please him, but because I actually wanted to drink the wine that came from my land, from my vines."

"And he was pleased?"

"To my surprise he offered me the '74 – our best year, of which there is very little left. It is matured and is a wine fit for the most discerning connoisseur."

"Surely that is a good sign?" Larisa suggested. "Perhaps after all he will agree to buy the vineyard you want so much."

"I have to go back to Paris tomorrow," the *Comte* said, "but I shall return the following day. I shall still have five days left in which to raise the money to buy the vineyard myself if my father refuses to do so."

"Perhaps he really has not got the money."

"It would be very easy for him to borrow what he wishes from the bank," Comte Raoul answered.

He turned again from his contemplation of the *Château* to look at her.

"And now let us talk about you," he said in a different tone of voice.

"I think I . . . must go back," Larisa said quickly.

"You are running away? Are you afraid of me?"

"I do not know at the . . . moment," Larisa replied. "Please do not . . . frighten me."

"I have no wish to do that," he said. "At the same time, I want to tell you how unbelievably lovely you are and how different from every other woman I have known."

His eyes were on her face and although she tried not to do so, irresistibly she looked at him and was unable to look away.

"I know that sounds trite," he said in a low voice, "but it is true. You are different, and what is happening between us is different."

"How can you be sure?" Larisa asked. "Here in the garden everything seems . . . unreal. Because it is evening and because . . ."

" . . . because we are together!" the *Comte* finished softly. "Do you realise where we are sitting, Larisa?"

He used her Christian name for the first time and, while she noticed it, she somehow could not protest.

"The Temple above us," the *Comte* went on as she did not speak, "is dedicated to Venus and the statues grouped around it are all of her in her different guises and under her different names."

He smiled and went on,

"Behind us is Aphrodite. She has always been my favourite ever since I was a small boy. That is why I brought you here tonight, so that we could talk together beneath Aphrodite, the Greek Goddess of Love."

His voice seemed to linger on the last word. Larisa felt herself thrill. It was like a streak of lightening running through her.

"I must not . . . listen to . . . you," she said.

"Why not?"

"Because I promised Mama I would not listen to compliments or believe anything a Frenchman might say to me."

"That was very sensible advice!" the *Comte* said, "but not where you and I are concerned."

"Why?"

"Because as I have already told you this is different!"

There was a depth and a warmth in his voice that made Larisa feel as if she vibrated to every word he said.

It was almost as if he touched her and yet he had not moved.

After a moment he said,

"Have you ever been kissed, Larisa?"

"No . . . of course not!" she answered quickly.

"Then it was meant for me to be the first," he said, "just as it was meant for us to meet and know that we belong to each other."

His voice deepened.

"But because what is between us is different from anything that has happened to me before, or to you, my beautiful little Aphrodite, I am not going to kiss you tonight."

His eyes were on her lips. Larisa felt a strange sensation sweep through her, something she had never felt or known before, something that was so exciting she felt herself tremble, at the same I time so intense that it was almost a pain.

Abruptly Comte Raoul rose to his feet.

"Come," he said. "I will take you back."

Larisa rose automatically.

Just as they had climbed in silence from the *Château* up to the statue of Aphrodite, so they returned without speaking.

She was vividly conscious of him and she knew that he was thinking of her in some manner she did not understand, compelling her to his will.

She felt almost as if he drew her into his arms, yet at the same time the control he had over himself held her apart for reasons she could not comprehend.

They reached the footbridge over the moat. The window of the Blue Cabinet was open just as they had left it.

Now the daylight had gone. There was only the twilight around them and the first stars were coming out overhead in the darkness of the sky.

Comte Raoul stopped and stood looking at Larisa.

Her eyes were wide and a little bewildered as she looked up into his.

"You are all a man could ever dream of and pray for," he said in his deep voice.

She felt herself quiver at his words and then he added,

"I am going for a walk in the woods to think about you. I have the feeling that you too will be thinking about me. That is all I ask for the moment – that you should think about me. Do you promise to do so?"

"I think it would be . . . difficult . . . not to," Larisa replied almost in a whisper.

"That is all I ask," he said. "Goodnight, my lovely goddess. We have found each other – that is the first step."

He took her hand as he spoke and for a moment Larisa felt his lips warm and insistent against her skin. Then almost before she could feel herself thrill at his touch he turned away and walked across the lawn into the shadow of the trees.

When he was out of sight slowly Larisa crossed the stone bridge and entered the *Château*.

As she went upstairs her whole mind was in a turmoil.

She could not think. She could not begin to understand what had happened.

It was so unexpected. Something she had never imagined, and as Comte Raoul had said, so very different from anything she had anticipated.

How could he be like this, so serious and yet be the same man who had been described as *"Monsieur le Diable"*? It did not make sense unless he was speaking the truth.

But how could she believe him?

She remembered what her mother had said to her, how Nicky had warned her, and most of all how Madame Madeleine had said it would be a disaster for her to meet Comte Raoul.

When she reached her bedroom, she sat down to think over what had happened, to try to understand it.

He had, she supposed, made love to her and yet it was not what she had expected love-making would be.

He had paid her compliments and yet they had not been the sort of compliments that she had thought would make her embarrassed or afraid.

Her body had vibrated to everything he had said.

She felt as if she understood what he was trying to say and it was so much deeper and more passionate than anything that could be expressed.

Then suddenly she felt very young, inexperienced and unsophisticated.

What did she know about love – if it was love?

How did she know what a man like Comte Raoul would say to a woman who he thought attractive?

Perhaps this was some rather clever approach that would make her intrigued and excited by him, a technique he had used before and found it was successful.

Then she told herself that was not true.

This was not the flirtatious overture of an experienced heartbreaker. He had been speaking with a sincerity that was undeniable.

There had been in some way a note of pain beneath his voice she could not quite explain.

She put her hands up to her face.

Her cheeks were flushed and she knew that ever since she had been with Comte Raoul her heart had been beating tumultuously against her breast.

She had felt too a strange constriction in her throat, and yet it had been a wonder beyond anything she had ever experienced before.

'Why does he make me feel like this?' she asked herself and would not face the answer.

She undressed and got into bed, but it was to lie awake thinking of Comte Raoul, being sure that he was thinking of her, drawing her thoughts so that she could not escape from him.

'I must be sensible!' Larisa told herself.

And yet she knew there was nothing sensible in the feelings that rippled through her and the chaos that existed within her mind.

An irrepressible ache made her yearn for the morning to come quickly so that she could see him again.

*

Larisa took Jean-Pierre downstairs for his morning walk earlier than usual.

She tried to tell herself she was hurrying because the sun was shining and it would be good for Jean-Pierre to get out in the fresh air.

But she knew in her heart that she was hoping Comte Raoul would be waiting for them.

As they came down the great staircase, Jean-Pierre holding Max on a lead, it was to find Monsieur le Comte standing in the hall taking his stick from one of the footmen.

He looked up as they approached.

There was a faint smile on his lips as he contemplated his grandson.

"Max is going a walk, *Grand-père*," Jean-Pierre said.

"So I see," Monsieur le Comte replied. "Is he a well-behaved dog?"

He looked at Larisa as he spoke and she answered,

"He is very good, *Monsieur*, and Jean-Pierre is very fond of him."

"Then see he does no damage to the treasures in my house," Monsieur le Comte said.

He spoke pleasantly and Larisa said quickly,

"We never let him off the lead except in the schoolroom, *Monsieur*."

Monsieur le Comte took Jean-Pierre by the hand and led him out of the front door and down the steps.

"This is Valmont, your home, Jean-Pierre," he said in an impressive tone. "The gardens are yours – the land is yours – it all belongs to you!"

"Max wants to run, *Mademoiselle*," Jean-Pierre said having apparently not heard his grandfather.

"He can run when you get into the woods," Larisa replied quickly. "Listen to what your grandfather is saying to you."

"He is too young to understand," Monsieur le Comte said, "but one day he will."

He relinquished the boy's hand and walked away moving slowly with his shoulders back and very upright.

'He is like a soldier going into battle,' Larisa found herself thinking.

Jean-Pierre was running off with Max in another direction and she followed quickly after him.

The day seemed to pass slowly.

It was difficult to concentrate on Jean-Pierre, to tell him stories, to try and make him absorb just one or two of the things she was trying to teach him.

Larisa found herself thinking so vividly of Comte Raoul that it was as if he was there beside her.

She went back over their conversation of last evening, and although she was shocked at her own feelings she knew, if she was honest, she had wanted him to kiss her.

'How can I be so fast or think in such a reprehensible manner?' she questioned.

But her practical common-sense seemed to have left her and all she could think of was the expression in his eyes and the note in his voice which evoked strange and exciting emotions.

At last, when Jean-Pierre had finished his supper, Suzanne took him off to bed and Larisa went to her own room.

She started to change, taking off the gown she had worn during the day and choosing another pretty muslin she had made herself from the wardrobe.

She had just put it down on the bed preparatory to washing, when there came a knock at the door, and before she could answer Nurse came into the room.

Larisa took one look at her face and said,

"What is the matter? What has happened?"

In answer Nurse shut the door behind her and then she burst into tears, the deep, half-strangled, frightening tears of the elderly.

"What is the matter? What has upset you?" Larisa asked. She put out her arms and drew the old woman across the room and into an armchair. Then she knelt down beside her saying,

"Tell me. *Please* tell me. I cannot bear you to be so unhappy."

"My baby! *My poor baby!*" Nurse cried.

"Has there been an . . . accident?" Larisa asked.

She knew who Nurse always referred to as 'her baby', and she felt as if an icy hand had been placed on her heart and it was difficult to speak.

"How could one think . . . how could one believe . . . that a father could plan anything so wicked?"

Larisa was suddenly still.

"What has Monsieur le Comte done?"

"I can't tell . . . you," Nurse sobbed, "no-one must know . . . but oh, my baby! My poor baby!"

Larisa drew a deep breath and then deliberately she reached out and taking the nurse's wrists drew her hands from her face.

"Tell me!" she said almost fiercely. "Tell me what has happened! I have to know!"

The tears were running down the nurse's cheeks and her mouth was trembling.

"Bernard was . . . boasting of it downstairs. I heard him . . . but he didn't know that I was listening."

"What was Bernard saying?" Larisa asked.

"I can't . . . tell you," Nurse whispered. "Perhaps it's not . . . true. My baby! *My baby!* I love him so much!"

"Tell me what you have heard!" Larisa insisted and now it was a command, an order.

Although Nurse struggled feebly, she could not release her wrists.

For a moment Larisa thought she would not speak, then suddenly she capitulated in a burst of tears.

"The wine!" she sobbed, "The wine is . . . *poisoned!*"

Larisa let Nurse's hands go free and said, her voice sounding strange even in her own ears,

"Monsieur le Comte intends him to die?"

"He's always . . . hated him!" Nurse cried "but I could not believe a man would . . . kill his own . . . son!"

Larisa rose to her feet.

She could not comprehend for a moment what she heard had actually been spoken.

It was incredible! Unbelievable! Something that could not be contemplated that a man like Monsieur le Comte could actually seek to destroy his only child.

Then she remembered the fanatical note in his voice when he had said,

"Jean-Pierre will take my place. Valmont will be his!"

He was mad!

But that would not save Comte Raoul!

As she thought of him, she knew what she must do.

She turned again to the sobbing woman.

"Listen, Nurse," she said, "I must save Comte Raoul and you have to help me!"

Her words arrested the tears and the nurse looked up at her.

"What can . . . you do, *M'mselle?*" she asked.

"I am going to Paris," Larisa answered, "I will warn him, but no-one must know I have gone. If I go to the stables, will they tell Monsieur le Comte?"

Nurse's breath was coming in little jerks between her lips, but she was no longer crying.

"Ask for Leon, you can trust him," she said. "Do not say where you are going. The Head Grooms will have gone home! There will only be Leon and some stableboys on duty. Just tell Leon you wish to go for a ride."

"I will do that," Larisa said, "and you must tell Suzanne and the housemaids who do my room that I have a headache and must not be disturbed."

She went to the wardrobe as she spoke and found a habit she had brought with her to France.

Her own, which had been passed down to her by Cynthus, was far too old and threadbare but she had taken her mother's which was only four years old.

It was made in the new fashion of a riding bodice and was particularly suitable for summer wear.

It was black with a touch of white at the neck and it fitted Larisa like a second skin. The skirt was wide and looked very elegant when it fell from the pummel and covered the stirrup.

The high-crowned hat that her mother had worn when out hunting was simple and yet smart.

Larisa swept back her hair from her forehead and pinned it tightly into a chignon so that it would not become untidy at whatever speed she travelled.

In a drawer she found a purse, her riding gloves and a thin, silver-handled whip that her father had given her on one of her birthdays.

Nurse had hooked her bodice up the back and now was standing watching her, the tears still wet on her cheeks.

"Now I have to get out of the *Château* without being seen," Larisa said.

"I will show you the way," Nurse answered.

They slipped out of the bedroom having seen there was no-one outside, Nurse locked the door and put the key into her pocket. '

They crept along the passages and Larisa realised that Nurse was taking her through a part of the *Château* that was not in use.

Finally after walking what seemed a very long way they reached the north wing and Nurse let Larisa out through a door that was only a very short distance from the stables.

"Ask for Leon," Nurse whispered, "and may *le Bon Dieu* bless and keep you."

"Pray that I may find Monsieur Raoul in time," Larisa replied.

She too spoke in a whisper then she turned and ran the intervening space between the *Château* and the stables.

A quarter of an hour later she was riding across the fields in what she knew was the direction of Paris.

It had been surprisingly easy.

Leon had understood when she told him she wanted to go for a ride, so he saddled a spirited horse for her which she knew would carry her swiftly but at the same time was not too hard for her to hold.

Larisa could ride well, but Monsieur le Comte's horses were better bred than those her father had been able to afford even in the days when he had seemed comparatively wealthy.

If she had not been so frightened of what lay ahead and agitated about Comte Raoul, she would have enjoyed the sensation of having the magnificent horse beneath her, knowing that the animal, because he was well trained, responded to her touch.

But for the moment she was concerned only with reaching Paris and when she did so of finding the *Comte*.

Supposing she was too late!

She found it impossible to think of him dead! He was so vitally, compellingly alive.

She thought of the deep note in his voice when he had talked to her last night, the feeling of his lips against her hand!

Then she could only see his debonair, expressive face, the way his dark hair grew back from his forehead, the faint smile on his lips.

She had met him yesterday for the first time but now she felt he had always been in her thoughts and in her life.

He was right – they had been meant to meet! It was Fate and perhaps too it was Fate that she should save him!

She spurred her horse so that he moved faster! She must be in time!

She knew where Comte Raoul lived because Madame Savigny, in talking of the different districts of Paris, had said that the *Champs-Élysées* was the most fashionable.

"Needless to say, Raoul lives there," she had said with a touch of pride in her voice. "At No. 24 next to the fantastic mansion that was built for La Marquise de Piava."

Larisa had never heard of the most extravagant, depraved and acclaimed courtesan of the Second Empire, who had scandalised Paris before the German occupation in 1871.

But she had remembered the number of the *Comte*'s apartment and she thought when first she saw the lights of Paris in the distance it would not be too hard to find the *Champs-Élysées*.

But there were more streets in the suburbs than she had anticipated and she had to ask her way a dozen times.

Finally she emerged at the top of the *Champs-Élysées* and saw the brilliantly lit avenue sloping away in front of her down to the *Place de la Concorde*.

After that it was not hard to find No. 24 and when she dismounted a small, ragged boy came forward and offered to hold her horse.

She pulled at the iron bell beside the impressive-looking door and impatiently raised her hand to the knocker.

It was opened by a servant wearing the Valmont livery.

"I wish to see Comte Raoul."

"*Monsieur* is not at home, *Madame*."

"Not at home?" Larisa repeated.

She had somehow expected it, but it was still a blow.

Then where is he?" she enquired.

She knew he had a party because he had told her so, but she had imagined he would be entertaining in his own house.

"I'm not certain, *Madame*, where *Monsieur* will be," the servant replied, "but I have an idea he was going first to the *Folies Bergères* and then perhaps to *Maxim's*."

"You are sure that is where I would find him?"

"I am almost sure, *Madame*."

"Is the *Comte's* valet here?" Larisa asked, remembering the man who had come with Comte Raoul to the *Château* and looked after Max in the phaeton.

"No, *Madame*. Henri is out."

Larisa stood on the doorstep indecisive.

What should she do?

Should she wait for Comte Raoul?

At the same time if he had a party, he might be drinking the wine.

When Comte Raoul returned from the country today," she said to the servant, "he brought with him a case of wine. Do you know what happened to it?"

"No, *Madame*, I was not on duty when *Monsieur* returned."

He frowned as if in concentration and added,

'But I heard *Monsieur* speaking of some special wine he required at his party tonight. I cannot remember what was said but I thought that he was choosing the menu."

Larisa's heart gave a frightened leap.

"I must find him!" she exclaimed. "Do you think as late as this he will still be at the *Folies Bergères*?"

She had no idea of the time but she thought it must be nearly 11 o'clock.

"Oh yes *Madame*" the servant answered, "the *Folies Bergères* does not finish until after midnight."

~132~

"Then I must go there," Larisa said. "Will you please arrange for my horse to be taken to the stables and call me a *voiture?*"

The servant looked faintly surprised but Larisa had the feeling that he had been asked to do stranger things while he had been in the service of Comte Raoul.

A groom was summoned from the stables, which were at the back of the house, a *voiture* was brought to the door and she stepped into it.

"Tell the *cocher* to drive to the *Folies Bergères* as quickly as possible!" she said.

As the man whipped up his horse she was thankful to remember that she had put her purse into the pocket of her riding habit.

If Comte Raoul had already left the *Folies Bergères* she would have to go on to the restaurant where he was having supper.

Now they were driving down the *Champs-Élysées*.

Unlike Larisa's curiosity about the city when she had arrived at the *Gare du Nord*, she was not now interested in looking out of the carriage windows. She tidied her hair with her hands, sweeping it back smoothly under her hat and wondering what Comte Raoul would say when he saw her so unexpectedly, and in a riding habit, when all his guests would be in evening dress.

But it was not important what he thought or did not think, Larisa decided.

All that mattered was that she should find him before he drank the wine his father had poisoned.

She had thought as she rode towards Paris that it was incredible and unbelievable that Monsieur le Comte, in his hatred of his son, should stoop to anything so bestial as murder.

But at the same time she was sure that what Nurse had overheard was the truth.

Bernard was a dark, rather sinister-looking man who Larisa had encountered a number of times in the passages and who had seemed almost to resent returning her polite greetings.

She thought now he was not only surly but there was something furtive about him.

He reminded her of a mediaeval servant who would follow out his master's commands whatever they might be.

The *voiture* had moved away from the wide boulevards and was travelling, Larisa realised along narrow, rather sordid streets.

She looked ahead of her apprehensively, until at last she saw night lights on the left-hand side of the road and a moment later the *voiture* came to a standstill.

There seemed to be a great many people on the pavement outside an entrance illuminated with electric bulbs and plastered with posters of women kicking their legs high in a manner that Larisa thought was indecent.

Suddenly she felt shy and embarrassed. How could she enter such a place – and alone?

Then she told herself it was of no consequence.

She had to find Comte Raoul, for once he had left the *Folies Bergères* she might never be able to get in touch with him again.

She stepped out of the *voiture*, paid the *cocher* and pushed her way through the gaping crowd.

They stared at her with curiosity. One man made a remark in a coarse voice that she did not understand but which evoked a roar of laughter from those standing near him. Inside an *entresol* separated from the theatre by glass doors, was a high desk at which two men were seated.

Larisa went up to one of them.

"Pardon, Monsieur," she said, "but I have to speak with Comte Raoul de Valmont, and I understand he is here. I have a message for him of the utmost importance.

"A message, *Madame?"* one of the men replied.

Larisa thought there was a rather cheeky expression on his face as he raised one eyebrow as if questioning her reasons for seeking Comte Raoul.

"It is a matter of life and death!" Larisa said.

She spoke so firmly that the man was obviously impressed.

He called a waiter wearing a silver-buttoned uniform.

"Escort this lady to Comte Raoul de Valmont," he ordered. *"Monsieur* is in his usual box."

"Come this way, *Madame,"* the waiter said and Larisa followed him into what, although she did not realise it, was the famous promenade of the *Folies Bergères*.

Very large, open, and with a long bar on one side of it, there was also a profusion of small tables at which sat flamboyantly and fantastically dressed women.

They all wore huge hats mostly trimmed with coloured feathers. There were feather boas around their shoulders and jewels glittering on their naked chests.

There were many men in evening dress and wearing their top hats and a great number unchanged but all wearing hats.

Larisa followed the waiter through the crowd where there seemed to be a great number of women alone.

Their eyelashes were heavy with mascara, their lips vividly red and they were looking boldly at the men with an invitation in their eyes.

Larisa saw as she advanced that at the far end of the promenade there was a theatre and on the stage a performance was taking place.

The music, which seemed to rise with difficulty above the sound of chattering and laughing voices in the promenade, was very energetic.

Just like the posters outside, the women on the stage were kicking their legs high in the air, showing their lacey white petticoats as they did so.

There was little time however for her to take everything in.

She had to move swiftly to keep up with the waiter in front of her as he pushed his way through the hordes of men who were leaning over a rail to watch the performance on the stage.

They went up several steps and now moved behind what appeared to be private boxes, built round and slightly higher than the stalls.

They were divided from each other with low partitions, very unlike the enclosed curtain-draped boxes of conventional theatres.

The waiter stopped at the box nearest the stage and now with a leap of her heart Larisa saw the man she had, come to seek.

He was alive! He was there!

He was sitting at the front of the box watching the performance and beside him were two of the most attractive women she had ever seen in her life.

Both were dark and one was wearing a red gown and a hat trimmed with red ostrich feathers to match. The other was in yellow with two great birds of Paradise sweeping back from her hat to nestle against her naked shoulders.

"Wait here, *Madame*," the waiter said to Larisa.

He moved forward pushing past the other people who filled the box to stand at the *Comte's* shoulder.

He bent and whispered in his ear.

Comte Raoul looked up and Larisa thought for a moment there was an expression of annoyance on his face as if he resented being disturbed.

Reluctantly he rose to his feet and apologised to his companions.

The lady in red put her hand on his arm and Larisa could see her face as she raised it towards Comte Raoul.

She was lovely, but her lips pouting provocatively were crimson and her eyelashes very artificially darkened.

Comte Raoul said something to make her laugh then he followed the waiter, speaking to two of his friends as he passed them in the box.

It was only as he stepped outside the low door that he saw Larisa.

He stared at her for a moment incredulously. Then as she found it hard to speak he asked,

"What are you doing here? What has happened?"

Before she could reply, Comte Raoul realised that the waiter who had escorted her to the box was waiting.

He drew a coin from his pocket and put it in the man's hand.

Then he took Larisa by the arm and drew her away from the box and against a wall.

"How have you got here?" he asked.

"I . . . rode."

"Alone?"

"I had to . . . see you! I had to . . . tell you something!"

He looked down at her riding-habit then back at her pale, anxious face.

"I can hardly believe that you are here," he said. "Tell me what has brought you?"

"The wine you brought from Valmont this morning," Larisa said, "it is . . . poisoned!

For a moment the *Comte* stared at her as if she had taken leave of her senses. Then he said quietly,

"You rode here alone from Valmont to warn me?"

"I was so afraid you might drink it and . . . die!" Larisa said.

"So you came to save me?"

"Yes."

She looked into his eyes as she spoke and for a moment she felt as if the crowded theatre, the noise and the music, everything disappeared.

They were alone, two people reaching out to each other across time and eternity.

Then the *Comte* said,

"Wait here."

He went back to the box.

A gentleman sitting on the back seat stood up to speak to him.

They spoke for some seconds and watching him Larisa saw the man nod his head as if he understood.

Then Comte Raoul came back to her and taking her by the arm said quietly,

"You must tell me all about it, then I will take you home."

CHAPTER SIX

Comte Raoul led Larisa back from the theatre into the promenade.

He walked her quickly past the women with their fantastic hats and the men standing against the bar with drinks in their hands who were flirting with the attractive, fair-haired bar maid who had been immortalised some years earlier in a picture by Manet. In the doorway he gave an order to one of the porters who hurried out into the street and in a few minutes reappeared to say,

"The carriage is waiting, *Monsieur.*"

Comte Raoul tipped him and led Larisa onto the pavement as a very smart closed carriage drew up with the coachman and footman wearing the Valmont livery.

The door was opened and Comte Raoul helped her in.

He then gave some long instructions to the footman, which she could not overhear, after which he sat down beside her and the door was closed.

For the first time Larisa felt shy at what she had done.

When she had heard at Valmont that he might die from the poisoned wine it had seemed right as well as imperative that she should ride to Paris to save his life.

Now that he was no longer in danger she was suddenly conscious of her own audacity in taking such a step and she also felt embarrassed at having taken him away from his party.

Was she being a nuisance to him? she wondered. How could she efface herself so that he need not concern himself with her any further?

"Did you have any dinner before you left?" the *Comte* asked. He spoke in a quiet matter-of-fact tone as if he sensed her rising agitation.

"No," she replied, "I was just changing when Nurse came to my bedroom."

"That is what I thought," he said, "and so before I take you back we will have supper together."

"There is no need for you to come with me," Larisa said quietly. "My horse is in your stables in the *Champs-Élysées* and I can easily find my own way."

By the light of the streetlamps she could see a smile on his lips as he answered,

"Do you really think I would let you go alone? It was very brave and very wonderful of you to undertake such a journey unattended. Incidentally how did you find my house?"

"It was more difficult than I thought," Larisa answered. "Paris is so big and there are so many small streets on the outskirts that I got lost at least half a dozen times."

"I am going to thank you for being so courageous," Comte Raoul said quietly, "but first you must have something to eat and drink. I suspect you are tired."

There was a caressing note in his voice, which made her feel protected in a way that she had never been before.

She had the feeling that it would be very easy to put her head on his shoulder and tell him how frightened she had been that she would not be in time.

Now the tension had passed she felt not only a little tired but also both limp and helpless.

The two horses that drew the carriage were moving quickly and before there was time to say more, they drew up in a pretty square where there were shrubs and trees in blossom and Larisa saw that they had stopped outside a small restaurant.

There was a striped awning over the door and the light from the windows was streaming out over the pavement.

"It is not *smart*, is it?" Larisa asked nervously, in a low voice as the footman opened the door. "I shall look very strange wearing a riding habit and I would not wish you to be ... ashamed of me."

"I should not be ashamed of you wherever we went," Comte Raoul said firmly, "but this is a very quiet place because I wish you to be able to talk to me freely."

Larisa stepped out onto the pavement, still feeling apprehensive until Comte Raoul led her into the restaurant. Then she saw he had spoken the truth when he said it was quiet.

It was also very small and divided into what amounted to two rooms where the diners sat on sofas against the walls and there was only just enough space for the waiters to move between the tables.

There were flowers everywhere and on the walls were strange, unusual pictures, which, Larisa guessed, had been painted by the much criticised and controversial Impressionists.

An elderly woman came forward beaming at the sight of Comte Raoul.

"This is an honour, *Monsieur!*" she exclaimed, "you have not visited us for some time."

"No, *Madame,* and tonight I want one of your most delicious dinners for someone who is very hungry."

"It will be a great pleasure, *Monsieur!*"

She led Comte Raoul and Larisa to a sofa-table situated in a corner and separated from the tables on each side of them by small banks of flowers.

As Larisa was about to sit down Comte Raoul said to her, "Why do you not take off your hat and be comfortable?"

"Can I do that?" she asked.

"Why not?" he enquired.

"If you come this way, *M'mselle*," the elderly woman said. She took Larisa to a cloakroom where she pulled off her riding hat.

She could not help wishing as she looked in the mirror that as she was dining with Comte Raoul, she could be wearing the white evening gown on which she and her mother had expended so much time and ingenuity.

She knew that the tight bodice and the soft lace around her shoulders had been very becoming. Instead, there was only the severity of her riding habit.

'I would like him to think me beautiful,' she told herself.

Then she remembered the women in his box at the *Folies Bergères* and thought that the comparison between them was laughable.

How he must resent being taken away from such alluring and exciting companions to feed a dull little governess who had never dined in a restaurant before!

How could she entertain him? What should she say?

She felt very ignorant!

When Larisa returned to the restaurant she had no idea how entrancingly her black habit accentuated the translucent clarity of her skin and threw into prominence the gold of her hair.

Her blue eyes were shy and there was a pleading look of apology in them as she seated herself beside the *Comte*.

He was, she thought, magnificent in his evening clothes. But because he was wearing them they seemed smarter and more elegant than they would have looked on any other man.

Then as his dark eyes met Larisa's, she felt herself quiver as she had done the night before and the breathlessness was back in her throat.

I will eat very quickly," she said, "and then you can go back to your party."

"I have no intention of joining them again," he answered. "I am going to take you back to Valmont, and I shall stay the night there."

"But your father . . . " she began hesitatingly.

"I want you to tell me exactly what has happened," the *Comte* said, "but before you do so I wish you to have something to eat, and especially some wine to drink."

As he spoke a *sommelier* brought a bottle of champagne to the table.

"It is, *Monsieur*, your usual Dom Perignon," he said, "and *Madame* thought tonight you would like a bottle of the '74. We have only a very little left."

At the mention of the date Larisa started.

"'74 was a great year for wine, especially champagne!" Comte Raoul explained.

The wine waiter poured a little of the golden liquid into a glass.

Comte Raoul tasted it.

"Excellent!" he said, "and just the right temperature!" Larisa's glass was half-filled and the *Comte* waited with a smile on his face for her to take a sip.

"It is delicious!" she exclaimed.

"The King of champagnes!" he answered. "Now drink a little more!"

Larisa did as she was told and felt the weakness that she suspected was mainly the result of shock disappearing. She knew now that the fear she had felt as she rode towards Paris had been in itself an insidious poison running through her until only now it had gone did she realise how intensely it had affected her.

"I suppose you know," Comte Raoul said as he set down his glass, "that it is an unheard of thing for a lady to visit the *Folies Bergères* alone?"

"There was nothing else I could do," Larisa answered simply. "I went first to your house and your servant said he was not certain where you were having supper, but he was almost sure that you would be at the *Folies Bergères*."

She paused and added in a low voice,

"I was so afraid of missing you and that I would be . . . too late."

"You thought the wine would be drunk at my party, which I told you I was giving?" Comte Raoul asked.

"Your servant said he heard you talking about wine when you were discussing the menu with someone, but he was rather vague about it."

"I would not have given the best Valmont wine to my guests tonight," Comte Raoul said.

He saw the expression on Larisa's face as she thought for a moment her ride had been unnecessary, and he added,

~145~

"But I might easily have had a glass of it by myself when I returned home before going to bed."

Larisa gave a little sigh and he went on,

"I very nearly opened a bottle when I was dressing for dinner. I do not know why, but I decided not to do so."

He smiled.

"It must have been just about the time you learnt that my life was in danger. Perhaps your thoughts or your prayers saved me!"

"I hope that was the reason," Larisa answered. "I was praying for you and so was Nurse."

"I am fortunate in having two such people to care for me."

The first dish Comte Raoul had ordered arrived, and while Larisa was eating and the waiters were serving them he began to talk in a different tone in an effort, she knew, to amuse her.

"Have you ever wondered," he asked, "why the famous theatre is called the *Folies Bergères*?"

"How did it get its name?" Larisa enquired.

"The theatre was named after the *Rue Bergères*, which in its turn was called after a master dyer who had his business there."

"It sounds rather prosaic!"

He smiled and went on,

"The term 'Folie' was used for many years to describe a piece of land where the soft grass and flowering bushes – were much favoured by romantic couples!"

He saw that Larisa was interested and continued,

"Later the word came to denote a public place where Parisians in the 18th century would dance, drink and watch entertainments in the open air."

"People talk about the *Folies Bergères* in England," Larisa said.

"And all over the world," Comte Raoul added. "It was the first music hall to be opened in Paris. I believe amongst its attractions was a woman with two heads and a magician who swallowed live snakes, ripped open his stomach and pulled out a rosary and pearls which he presented to ladies in the audience!"

Larisa laughed before she said,

"Many people tonight were not watching the stage, and there appeared to be lots of women unaccompanied."

The *Comte* did not answer for a moment and then he said,

"As I have already said, the *Folies Bergères* is not a place that a lady would visit alone or with anyone else!"

Larisa turned to look at him, her eyes wide.

"But you took your party there!"

"My guests were not like you."

She thought again of the beautiful ladies that he had beside him before the waiter who had taken her to the box had interrupted him.

The lady in red particularly who had put her hand on his arm had been so lovely and so exquisitely dressed that Larisa felt she could understand Comte Raoul's annoyance at being taken away from her company. As if he guessed the questions that were puzzling her he said quietly,

"I have many friends whom you must realise I would not invite to Valmont, nor would my Aunt Emilie receive them!"

Larisa hesitated for a moment and then she said,

"Madame Madeleine spoke of the . . . *'demi-monde'*. Is that what they . . . are?"

Comte Raoul smiled.

"It is a good word for them!"

"They are very pretty and attractive," Larisa said almost beneath her breath. "They make me feel very . . . dull and shabby by comparison."

"Do you really think that?" he asked. "Shall I tell you what I thought you looked like as you came back to the table just now having taken off your hat?"

Larisa did not answer but she raised her eyes to his.

"I thought you looked like the dawn when it sweeps away the darkness of the night, when just for that one moment there is the gold of the sun in the sky and at the same time the darkness with its fading stars is still there."

Larisa drew in her breath.

There was that note of sincerity in his voice, which made her feel that he was speaking the truth, which came from the very depths of his heart.

Then she dropped her eyes and looked away.

"Thank you," she murmured, "but you make me feel . . . shy."

"I adore you when you are shy," Comte Raoul said, "I had forgotten that a woman could blush or that eyes could be so innocent and childlike."

He paused and then he added,

"Oh, my dear, I wish you had not come to Paris tonight!"

"But why?" Larisa asked in consternation.

"Because I do not wish you to see anything that is ugly or sordid," he answered. "I wish you to remain as you are, looking like Aphrodite awakening to the beauty of love and ignorant of the sordid emotions that besmirch and deface something that is in reality Divine."

Larisa looked at him in bewilderment.

She did not understand what he was saying, and yet she knew that every word he spoke seemed to envelop her in a cloud of glory.

How could she have thought . . . how could she have imagined in her wildest dreams that Comte Raoul de Valmont – *'Monsieur Le Diable'* – would speak in such a manner?

She knew it was an unbelievable enchantment to be here alone with him as she had never been alone with a man before. But the things he said and the way in which he spoke them seemed to call not merely to her heart, but to her very soul.

She had always known that love, real love, would be part of God, but it was impossible to tell him so – and yet she felt he understood.

As the next course was being served, he said,

"Tell me about your home and your family."

Larisa started with her father's interest in Greece.

"That is why I smiled when you said I looked as if I came from Olympus," she told Comte Raoul. "My sisters and I can never get away from the Greek image."

"You have sisters?"

"Three."

"And they are as beautiful as you?"

"Papa called us his four Venuses."

"It is sheer cruelty to a mere man, but I would like to see them."

Larisa was silent then she said in a low voice,

"Perhaps if you saw Athene and Delos you would no longer admire me."

Comte Raoul looked at her for a long moment before he replied,

"Look at me, Larisa."

She turned her head obediently and met his eyes.

"Do you really think," he asked, "that what I feel for you depends entirely on your looks, breath-taking though they are?"

She could not answer and he went on,

"We both know that what we feel is far, far deeper than the superficiality of outward appearance."

Larisa drew in her breath.

"I adore your face, your blue eyes, your straight little nose, the curve of your lips," he continued. "But my heart responds to your heart, my soul to your soul. I feel the magnetism of your spirit, your character and your personality reaching out to mine. It is all part of my love."

Larisa felt herself quiver at what he said.

Yet she knew the actual words that came to his lips were not important.

It was what remained unsaid that vibrated between them and was like a magnet drawing them closer and still closer with every minute that passed.

She told him about her home and how she went to work to keep Nicky at Oxford, and she knew he understood.

Finally, when there were only two cups of coffee in front of them on the table, the *Comte* had a glass of brandy in his hand, and there were no longer any attentive waiters to interrupt them he said quietly,

"Now tell me exactly what has happened at Valmont?"

In a low voice Larisa explained how Nurse had come to her bedroom in a flood of tears and how she had overheard Bernard boasting that he had poisoned the wine on Monsieur le Comte's instructions.

"Nurse believed it to be the truth?"

"She was sure that Bernard had done what he said," Larisa answered.

"And you had no doubt in your mind that my father would do such a thing?"

Larisa paused for a moment and then she answered, "The first day I came, Monsieur le Comte spoke of Valmont belonging to Jean-Pierre and that the continuance of the family was centred only in him."

She felt this would hurt Comte Raoul but she went on,

"I thought then that he seemed to be ignoring the fact that you were in existence. Yet I was sure the estate must come to you before it could go to Jean-Pierre."

Her voice died away. Then as Comte Raoul did not speak she added,

"Later I asked Madame Savigny if it was not a fact that you would inherit Valmont when your father was dead."

"So you think he had been planning to get rid of me for a long time?" Comte Raoul asked.

"It seems impossible! Unbelievable! But his whole interest, the only thing he appears to care for is Jean-Pierre!"

"I know that," Comte Raoul answered, "but I did not think he would go as far as murder!"

"Because he has failed this time," Larisa said in little more than a whisper, "he may . . . try again!"

"That is of course a probability," Comte Raoul agreed.

She turned towards him, quickly.

"Then you must not come back to Valmont, it would be ... dangerous. You must stay in Paris!"

Comte Raoul squared his chin and for a moment his lips met in a hard line.

Then he said quietly,

"That is not the answer. This is something that has to be faced, to be fought out between my father and me."

It might be ... dangerous for you," Larisa insisted.

"It has already been dangerous," the Comte answered, "but you have saved me. Do you think I can forget for one moment that you rode alone to Paris to protect me?"

Again there was that note in his voice that made her quiver.

"Now I am taking you back," he went on. "Who knows that you have left the *Château*?"

"Nurse said that Leon was to be trusted. I told him I wished to go for a ride."

"Did he seem surprised?"

"No. I explained that I felt I needed some exercise and I had not asked permission of Monsieur le Comte to borrow one of his horses. I had the feeling, although I might be wrong, that he will not betray me."

"Let us hope you are right," Comte Raoul said. "I do not wish you to be involved in this. If my father suspects you are interested me or that you came to warn me, he would undoubtedly dismiss you!"

Larisa gave a little sound of dismay.

She knew that Comte Raoul spoke the truth, but it would be terrible to have to go back to England not knowing what was happening to him, not knowing the end of the drama in which despite of herself she was now closely associated.

Comte Raoul paid the bill and had risen to his feet when from the inner room of the restaurant a vision of loveliness appeared.

It was a woman with dark, flashing eyes and like the ladies in the theatre her lips were crimson and her eyelashes mascaraed.

She had red hair surmounted by a small hat trimmed with ospreys.

Her evening gown was very *décolleté* and the emeralds that encircled her long, white neck must have been worth a King's ransom!

She was about to leave through the outer door which was opened for her when she saw Comte Raoul.

She gave a little cry of delight and held out both her hands to him.

"Raoul! How delightful to see you!"

Comte Raoul raised first one of her hands, and then the other to his lips.

"Needless to say," he replied, "the pleasure is mine!"

"You have not been to see me for weeks, or is it months?"

"That is an omission I must undoubtedly correct, at the earliest opportunity."

"Please come!" she said softly, "I want to see you."

Before Comte Raoul could reply, the lady's escort, a middle-aged man, came to her side.

"I am waiting, Odette," he said.

"I am just coming!" Odette replied a little impatiently, then added, "Your Serene Highness knows Comte Raoul de Valmont?"

"We have met," the elder man said coldly.

"We have indeed, Your Serene Highness," Comte Raoul replied.

"Do not forget, Raoul, that I am expecting you," Odette said softly.

Then she took the arm of her escort and swept from the restaurant.

While they had been talking Larisa had not moved from her place at the table.

She could only watch and feel overwhelmed by the beauty, the loveliness and above all the sophistication of the woman talking with Comte Raoul.

She had been able to see the expression in her dark eyes when she looked at the *Comte*.

'She loves him!' Larisa told herself and knew the knowledge was like a pain in her breast.

Comte Raoul had his back to her so she had no idea what expression was on his face.

But she told herself that he could not help responding to anyone so alluring, so enticing.

She suddenly felt as if the restaurant had become very dark and all the excitement she had felt while they had been having dinner had gone, leaving a kind of emptiness and utter depression.

'How could I have imagined for one moment that he was interested in talking to me?' Larisa asked herself, 'when he could be with someone like that?'

She thought how drab and dull she must look despite what he had said to her.

Her lips must look so pale beside the warm crimson of Odette's and the other women with whom he had been sitting in the *Folies Bergères*.

No wonder he wished to come to a quiet restaurant when he was escorting a dull little governess in a black riding habit instead of someone in a Paris creation that revealed her white neck and shoulders.

As Comte Raoul turned back towards her, Larisa rose from the table and picked up her riding hat.

The first dinner she had ever had alone with a man was over!

It had been an hour of sheer delight when she had talked, listened and felt herself quiver to many strange emotions.

Now ahead there was only the long journey back to Valmont and the thought that she was taking Comte Raoul away from his amusements and the women who loved him.

"Monsieur has enjoyed his dinner?"

It was *Madame* bowing to them as they were ready to leave, and now the chef wearing the white hat of his calling came from the kitchen.

"You are satisfied, *Monsieur*?" he asked Comte Raoul.

"As usual everything was excellent and the wine superlative!" Comte Raoul answered.

"And *M'mselle*?" the chef enquired.

"It was the best dinner I have ever eaten!" Larisa said in a low voice.

Madame gave a little cry of delight.

"That is what we wish to hear," she said. "Please bring *M'mselle* to us again soon, *Monsieur*."

"I will do that," Comte Raoul replied.

Larisa wanted to add miserably it was something that would never happen.

Instead she forced herself to smile at the chef and *Madame*, then she followed Comte Raoul outside.

Instead of the carriage she had expected, there was waiting for them the *Comte's* phaeton drawn by two spirited horses which she had seen before outside the front door at Valmont.

The groom jumped down and Comte Raoul took his place and picked up the reins.

Larisa climbed into the seat next to him.

"You will bring my clothes down as soon as you get back." Comte Raoul said to the groom.

"I will do that, *Monsieur.*"

The groom saluted and they drove off.

'What about my horse?" Larisa asked, "or are we stopping at your house?"

"We cannot do that," Comte Raoul answered, "and your horse has already left for Valmont. He will be waiting for you in the drive when we arrive there."

"Why can we not stop at your house?" Larisa asked curiously.

"The answer is quite simple," Comte Raoul replied. "It is a bachelor establishment."

"Do you mean that no woman ever visits you there?"

He smiled.

"I would not say that, but certainly not one of the *Beau Monde.*"

Larisa was silent digesting what he had said.

She was glad he included her in the *Beau Monde*. At the same time, it seemed that the *demi-monde* enjoyed special privileges that were forbidden to her.

She thought of the women she had seen with Comte Raoul this evening and found herself wishing that she too could be of the *demi-monde*.

How hard it must be to resist the wiles and the loveliness of such women, how easy to be bored with what Madame Savigny had described as the *ancien régime* who would not go to the *Folies Bergères* or any other of the Parisian nightspots, but sat in their houses disapproving of everyone else.

It was not surprising, Larisa thought, that someone like Comte Raoul found the bright lights of the new Paris more amusing and more entertaining than the life in which he had been brought up.

Valmont might be beautiful, but he had described it as a 'cemetery'.

He was young, debonair, dashing and adventurous!

Was it likely that he would want to spend years of his life thinking only of economy, grudging the expenditure of every penny, talking only to the few blue-blooded families like his own who thought everyone else vulgar and parvenu?

"I wish I was a man!" Larisa said aloud.

"I for one am exceedingly glad you are a woman!" he smiled, "but why this sudden desire for a change?"

"I was thinking how amusing your life here must be, even though some people consider it reprehensible," Larisa replied.

She paused and added in explanation.

"Madame Savigny explained to me how much your relations and their friends disapprove of all the new innovations, even of electric light!"

"And you really think my behaviour is more to be desired?" the *Comte* asked.

There was an irony in his voice and Larisa answered,

"Naturally I am not aware of the things you have done of which people disapprove so strongly but all men want to have fun and how indeed could you resist women who are so lovely or so enticing as those I saw you with tonight?"

"You sound as if you were a little jealous of them," the *Comte* said.

"It is not so much jealousy as envy," Larisa replied. "I suppose all women want to be beautiful and gorgeously dressed, to wear expensive jewels and have young men like you admiring them."

"Did I say I admired them?" Comte Raoul asked.

"It is obvious, is it not?" Larisa asked. "You asked the two ladies in your box to your party, and the lovely lady who spoke to you just now is very anxious to see you again."

Comte Raoul did not answer.

They were moving through the narrow streets of the suburbs.

In a few minutes Larisa knew they would be out of the city and into the open countryside.

She wondered why she worried about anything except the joy of being beside him, of watching him drive his horses with an expertise that she had never seen before, knowing that he was not only the most attractive man she had ever seen, but also the most attractive man in all Paris.

For the moment there were no beautiful women to tempt him or to distract his attention.

She was alone with him and she knew that this was a moment she would always remember.

'What is the point of talking?' she asked herself. 'There are no explanations and indeed no answers to all the questions that perplex me. I shall never understand his life and all I can do is to be grateful for whatever kindness he shows me, for the times that we can be together.'

How could she have dreamt, she thought, the day before yesterday that she would have a man like Comte Raoul talking to her of love or giving her dinner?

Even if she never saw him again, she knew that when they had sat together beneath the statue of Aphrodite and when he had taken her to the restaurant there were moments that she would never forget and which were hers for all eternity.

No-one could take those away from her whatever happened!

If she never saw him again it would still be something to remember, something to treasure, something that in some strange, inexplicable manner had become part of herself.

They drove on and she had the feeling that the *Comte* was pushing his horses a little and that he was in a hurry to reach Valmont.

Larisa tried not to think how hard it was going to be to leave him, to go into the house alone not certain what would happen to him or what Monsieur le Comte's reaction would be to his unexpected arrival.

She tried to tell herself it was none of her business.

But she knew that she was irrevocably and indivisibly a part of the terrible events taking place in the Valmont family and at the *Château*, so that she could no longer pretend she was an outsider or that they were nothing to do with her.

Now the woods that surrounded the Valmont Estate were appearing and they turned in at the high, wrought iron gates, which were surmounted by the family crest in stone.

They entered the long, lime tree-lined avenue but to Larisa's surprise the *Comte* drove his horses off the gravel and onto the grass verge and they travelled only a very short distance before he brought them to a standstill.

"Why are we stopping here?" Larisa asked. "Is your groom to meet us here with my horse?"

"No, I told him to wait at the bottom of the drive," Comte Raoul replied. "Then you can ride back to the stables and say you got lost, which was why you took so long to return."

As he spoke, he tied the reins to the dashboard in front of him, turned to Larisa, and put his arms around her.

"Before you leave me," he said softly, "I want to thank you for saving my life."

The moonlight, which had been struggling through the clouds ever since they left Paris, suddenly emerged in the clearness of the sky and, seeping through the darkness of the trees, shone on Larisa's face as she looked up at him.

She had the feeling that she ought to struggle and prevent him from drawing her close to him.

But somehow it seemed this was inevitable, something she had known would happen without actually being conscious of it.

"You are so lovely, my little Aphrodite!" she heard Comte Raoul say. "When you are there all other women look tawdry and as far as I am concerned unattractive!"

He felt a little quiver go through Larisa, then very gently he bent his head and found her lips.

For a moment his mouth hardly touched hers.

Then as he pressed her a little closer to him she felt a strange feeling like quicksilver streak through her body and an unbelievable ecstasy rise within her.

It was something she had never imagined.

It was a wonder that seemed to come from the moonlight itself and yet was a flame deep within her body.

Everything she knew, understood or thought disappeared into a feeling of being part of him and they were alone, away from the world, which no longer existed, in a starlit sky where there was only the beauty and wonder and a perfection that was part of Heaven.

How long his lips held her captive Larisa had no idea.

She only knew that every second the wonder within her seemed to deepen and quicken until when finally he raised his head and her lips were free, she could only look up at him and feel it was impossible even to breathe.

"*Le premier fois,* my lovely!" he said in a voice that was unsteady, "the first time for you and I swear to you the first time for me. Never before have I known a kiss to be like that or that it could mean a million wonders I did not even know existed!"

Because the note in his voice made her tremble with the sheer intensity of her feelings Larisa turned her head and hid it against his shoulder.

He drew her closer to him and then he said, his voice deep and a little hoarse,

"I told you we were different. Now do you believe me?"

She could not answer and after a moment very gently he put his fingers under her chin and turned her face up to his.

I love you!" he said, "and I did not know that love could be so completely overwhelming to the point where I can no longer think of anything but you!"

"How can you love . . . me?" Larisa asked a little doubtfully.

"That is a question I have asked myself," Comte Raoul answered. "I know all the arguments against such a thing happening, we have only just met, we do not know each other, we have lived in different worlds, but the fact remains that I love you! And I think that you already love me a little."

Shyly Larisa would have hidden her face again, but he would not let her.

"Tell me the truth, my darling," he said, "because although your lips have told me what you feel I also want to hear you say so."

"I . . . love you!" Larisa whispered, "but . . ."

"There are no buts," he interrupted. "Just for this moment at any rate think of nothing but our love."

He gave a deep sigh.

"The difficulties and problems ahead of us are unimportant besides our love. Tell me that is all that matters to you, that I love you and you love me?"

"I love . . . you," Larisa whispered again.

His lips were on hers and this time they were more insistent, more demanding, as once again she felt that wild ecstasy rise within her, and set her free.

"You must go back," he said, "I have kept you out late enough as it is. I do not wish you to have to make explanations."

Larisa made no answer.

She still felt as though every nerve in her body was throbbing with the rapture he had evoked in her.

He picked up the reins and the horses that had been standing still moved on.

As they went, Larisa put on her riding hat, which she had held in her hand all the time they had been driving from Paris.

She had only just set it in place when the horses reached the end of the drive and the *Comte* drew them once again to a standstill.

Standing in the shade of the trees Larisa saw the *Comte's* groom waiting with the horse on which she had ridden to Paris.

"Ride home, my darling," the *Comte* said in a quiet voice that only she could hear. "Go to bed and sleep. Do not worry about anything."

"What time will you be arriving?" Larisa asked.

"I shall wait a little while," he answered, "so that there will be no chance of anyone thinking we have been together."

There were a dozen questions Larisa wanted to ask him.

What would he say to his father? Would he confront him with his knowledge that the wine was poisoned? Would he ask Monsieur le Comte for an explanation?

But her horse was waiting with the groom beside him.

She stepped out of the phaeton and as she reached the horse's side the *Comte* followed her to lift her into the saddle.

His groom went to the heads of the horses pulling the phaeton and was out of earshot.

"You will be careful, will you not?" Larisa asked in a low voice.

"I shall remember that you saved me," he answered.

He arranged the skirt of her habit over the pummel and pulled it into place over the side of the horse.

There was something in the way he did it that gave Larisa a little thrill. He was looking after her, taking care of her, and she thought as she looked down at him how irresistibly attractive he was and how at the moment any woman in Paris would be glad to be in her position and receive his attentions.

The *Comte* took her hand and moving the edge of her driving glove from her wrist lifted it to his lips to kiss the little blue veins where they met in the palm.

"Goodnight, my only love!" he said gently. "I shall see you tomorrow."

He released her hand and without speaking Larisa turned her horse into the drive and rode towards the *Château* without looking back.

As she went, she was conscious that her lips were still throbbing from the touch of his and she could still feel his mouth against the veins on her wrist.

'I love him!' she told herself. *'Oh God, how much I love him!'*

CHAPTER SEVEN

Larisa and Jean-Pierre reached the top of the staircase and she saw with a start of excitement that Comte Raoul was below them in the hall.

It was a lovely day. Larisa was taking Jean-Pierre and Max for a walk but she had to be honest with herself and say that she had hurried over the schoolroom breakfast because she longed so desperately to see Comte Raoul again.

She had crept back into the house last night after leaving her horse in the stables with Leon and had thought everyone was asleep until she reached her bedroom to find Nurse dozing in an armchair.

She spoke and the old woman awoke with a start.

"It is all right!" Larisa said soothingly, "I was in time. He had not opened the wine."

She saw quick tears come to Nurse's eyes and knew how desperately afraid she must have been all the long hours when she had been afraid that no one could save the *Comte*.

"I was thinking of you, *M'mselle*," Nurse said in a low voice. "I should not have let you go off alone all that way by yourself, but you were the only person that could warn him."

"If I had not gone," Larisa said gently, "he told me that he might easily have drunk a glass of the wine before he went to bed."

"*Le Bon Dieu* is merciful!" Nurse exclaimed in a broken voice. "He has heard my prayers and I prayed both for my baby and for you."

"And we are both all right!" Larisa said soothingly.

Yet even as she spoke the question was there in her mind as to how long Comte Raoul would be safe.

But she was very tired and she had no wish to worry Nurse with such problems at the moment.

Instead, she let the old woman help her out of her riding habit and when she got into bed she fell asleep almost immediately from sheer exhaustion.

It was hard when she awoke to remember Comte Raoul was still in danger.

All she could think of was the wonder of his kiss, and the feeling of ecstasy when he had held her in his arms and told her that he loved her.

Nevertheless, Monsieur le Comte hovered over them like a bird of evil prey.

As she and Jean-Pierre descended the stairs Larisa was wondering if Comte Raoul had already seen his father and what they had said to each other at breakfast.

Then before they were halfway down a voice behind them made her jump.

"Good morning, Raoul! I heard that you arrived late last night."

It was Monsieur le Comte coming downstairs behind them and Larisa realised that he must have breakfasted in his bedroom and father and son had not yet met.

"Good morning, Father!" Comte Raoul replied. "I have been waiting to see you."

"So I was told," Monsieur le Comte said.

They all three stepped onto the marble floor of the hall.

"I wish to talk to you, Father," Comte Raoul said in a grave voice.

"And I shall be only too pleased to hear what you have to say to me," Monsieur le Comte explained. "But first I have something for you to do that is of the utmost importance."

"What is that?"

"I have been informed," Monsieur le Comte explained, "that a fox has taken two more of our lambs – that makes five in a week! This can continue no longer!"

"I should think not!" Comte Raoul said. "Surely Gascoyne is doing something about it?"

"Unfortunately," Monsieur le Comte replied, "Gascoyne has hurt his arm, and as you well know he is the only man I would trust with a gun on this part of the estate."

Comte Raoul did not reply and Monsieur le Comte went on,

"What I want you to do, Raoul, is to shoot the fox before it can do any more damage. The shepherd thinks that it is a vixen and has cubs, in which case they are doubtless in the sandpit at the top of the woods. The foxes have an earth there every year."

"Yes, I know they do," Comte Raoul replied. "And I cannot understand why Gascoyne has not seen to it earlier."

"He has been very short-handed," Monsieur le Comte explained, "but the foxes are playing havoc with the sheep. They are not only killing the young lambs but also frightening the ewes."

"I will see to it," Comte Raoul promised.

"I thought you would," Monsieur le Comte replied. "If not, I must do it myself."

"No, Father, it is too far for you to walk."

"I told Bernard to have a gun ready for you," Monsieur le Comte said. "I see it is there on the settle."

Comte Raoul walked across the hall to pick up the gun, which was lying on the settle, and slung a bag of cartridges over his shoulder,

"It should not take me long, Father," he said. "We will talk when I return."

"I will be waiting for you."

Comte Raoul turned towards the front door.

Just for a moment it seemed to Larisa that as he passed her his eyes lingered on her face.

She saw the expression in his eyes and felt as if he had touched her.

Then he was gone and she waited for Monsieur le Comte to speak to Jean-Pierre.

"What are you going to do this morning, Jean-Pierre?" Monsieur le Comte asked in the gentle voice he always used to his grandson.

Jean-Pierre was playing with Max and when he did not reply Larisa said,

"We are going for a walk, *Monsieur.*"

Monsieur le Comte seemed to hesitate and then he said,

"I do not wish you to do so this morning. My son will be shooting and Bernard is also setting up a gun trap. It would be best for you to stay in the house. This afternoon I will take Jean-Pierre for a drive."

"He would like that, *Monsieur,*" Larisa answered.

"We will make further plans at luncheon," Monsieur le Comte said.

He put his hand in a gesture of affection upon Jean-Pierre's head and then walked across the hall in the direction of the salon where he always sat.

"Take Max for a walk?" Jean-Pierre asked.

"No, not this morning," Larisa answered. "Your grandfather wishes us to stay in the house."

"Max wants a walk!" Jean-Pierre said obstinately. Larisa looked through the door at the sunshine outside and knew that she was as disappointed as Jean-Pierre was at being confined to the house.

Then she had an idea.

"Listen, Jean-Pierre," she said, "I will tell you what we will do. We will go to the roof. You have never shown me the view from there and you can point out to me all the special places in the garden and the woods where we have walked."

Jean-Pierre was only too delighted to show her the way up the stairs to the very top landing.

Then up a twisting, winding staircase in one of the turrets until they could step out onto a flat part of the roof which reached right to the cupola.

It had a beautiful wrought-iron railing around it so that it was completely safe.

Nurse had suggested several times that Larisa should see the view from the top of the *Château*.

It really was very impressive and she could see an immense distance in almost every direction.

She looked over the formal gardens to the Temple to Venus, and she could see the statue of Aphrodite under which she and Comte Raoul had sat.

She could look in the direction of Paris and recall how last night she had galloped frantically over the parkland and fields until she found the main road that led into the city.

Then because she could not help herself she looked down at the path where she knew Comte Raoul would walk towards the top of the wood. She could see him very clearly.

Already he had left the gardens, which were enclosed by a wall, and was passing through the grassland where the sheep were grazing.

They occupied only half of the field, which was partitioned off with hurdles, but it was bordered by the pine woods and it was from there, Larisa thought, the foxes must have crept out to snatch the baby lambs.

The path Comte Raoul was taking was cut through the centre of the wood and she could see him moving higher and higher to where she guessed the fox's den was likely to be.

A sudden sound behind her made her turn round.

Jean-Pierre already bored with looking at the view, was playing with Max.

At the moment he had both hands round the puppy's throat and was squeezing it so tightly that the dog was struggling frantically, obviously in pain.

"Jean-Pierre! Stop that immediately!" Larisa said sharply. "I have told you before that it hurts Max when you put your hands round his throat."

Reluctantly it seemed to her Jean-Pierre released the dog and there was an expression in his eyes that Larisa did not like.

This was the second time she had caught him trying to throttle the animal, and she knew with a sudden fear that she would have to speak to Monsieur le Comte about him.

He should see a doctor – she was sure of that!

Once again she could not escape from the memory of the village idiot at Redmarley who had strangled a little girl of three.

Max, apparently unaffected by the pain he had suffered, was wagging his tail and running about quite happy to play with Jean-Pierre, but Larisa found it impossible for the moment to forget the look in the little boy's eyes.

'Surely I am exaggerating something that, is just childish mischief?' she asked herself desperately.

Then she knew that she would have to discuss Jean-Pierre with someone.

She could not go on much longer pretending he was normal.

Because she felt so horrified by her own thoughts, she turned once again to look for Comte Raoul.

Just to think of him and to be able to see him in the distance was to make her feel calmer and less agitated.

He was out of sight but someone else had emerged from the garden into the field where the sheep were.

It was a man and Larisa was almost certain it was Bernard.

He did not interest her and she was looking once again in the distance for Comte Raoul when she suddenly saw Bernard walk across the field, bend over one of the hurdles and pick up a baby lamb.

He carried it back in his arms and when he was about ten yards from the path that led to the woods he put it down.

Watching, Larisa realised it had disappeared!

For the moment she was surprised, then, she knew Bernard must have set it down in a hole which was why she could not now see it. Only half curiously, because her thoughts were really on Comte Raoul, she saw Bernard place something dark down in the grass and cover the dark object with it.

Suddenly Larisa understood!

It must be the gun trap of which Monsieur le Comte had spoken!

She had heard of them although she had never seen one at close quarters.

She had an idea that they were sometimes used in England, but more often in foreign countries where savage animals were dangerous to children or crept up at night to native villages ready to kill anything that moved.

Bernard had obviously finished what he had come to do.

Now he turned and hurried back into the garden, only pausing as he reached the gate in the wall that led into the field to look back over his shoulder.

He looked not in the direction of the gun trap, but up the path along which Comte Raoul had walked to the fox's den.

He looked for a moment and then turned away and Larisa saw that he was running back to the *Château*.

She thought it strange that he should be in such a hurry. Perhaps Monsieur le Comte wanted him. Then suddenly she understood!

The trap Bernard had set was not for the fox, but for Comte Raoul!

No fox was likely to walk down the path from the woods or to approach, not at any rate in the daytime, a trap that was so far from the shelter of the trees.

But Comte Raoul would return down the path to enter the garden the way he had left it and as he passed he would hear the bleating of the lamb that had been put in the hole.

It was obvious that he would go to investigate what was happening and Larisa was certain that the gun would be aimed not so as to kill a fox but, at the height of a man's heart.

She was so certain that her supposition was right, that the realisation of what Monsieur le Comte had planned seemed to hit her like a physical blow.

She could only hold onto the railing in front of her and feel helpless and unable to think of what she should do.

Then she knew she must warn Comte Raoul.

Once again she must save him.

"Come, Jean-Pierre," she said insistently, "we have to go and find your father."

"Max go for a run?" Jean-Pierre asked.

"Yes, we will take Max for a run," Larisa answered.

For a moment she had thought of leaving Jean-Pierre and Max in the schoolroom.

Then she knew that would invite questions.

How could she run off on her own across the garden and up into the wood without the child who was supposed to be in her charge?

No, she would take Jean-Pierre with her and if Monsieur le Comte questioned her as to why she had disobeyed his order, she would have to think of some excuse.

At the moment the only thing that mattered was to save Comte Raoul.

She hurried Jean-Pierre down from the roof and they descended the back stairs which were nearest to the side of the *Château* where she wished to emerge.

The door that led into the garden was open and, taking Jean-Pierre's hand, Larisa ran towards the gate that led into the field.

It seemed to take much longer when they were down below than she had expected it would when she had looked down on from the roof.

They were both rather breathless by the time they reached the gate in the wall.

Larisa pulled it open.

As she did so she heard the lamb bleating just as she had expected, crying for its mother from whom it had been taken.

"Come along, Jean-Pierre," Larisa said, "we will go and find your father."

They walked along the path and the lamb's bleating cry sounded piteous to Larisa although it did not seem to concern Jean-Pierre.

They walked the whole length of the field and entered the wood.

Larisa looked doubtfully ahead.

How could she be sure that Comte Raoul would return the same way he had gone?

Suppose he came back by another route?

She stood still, undecided as to what she should do.

Max was dragging at his lead anxious to run into the wood and Jean-Pierre pulled at her hard.

"Come on, *Mademoiselle*."

The only thing she could do, Larisa thought rather helplessly, was to keep looking back into the field in case she should see Comte Raoul emerge from the wood from a different direction.

Then even as she worried and turning her head felt hopelessly undecided, she heard someone moving through the trees.

To her utter relief she saw Comte Raoul coming towards them.

"There he is!" she exclaimed with a note of joy in her voice. "There is your father, Jean-Pierre!"

As if her enthusiasm animated, the small boy he let go of her hand and ran through the pine trees towards Comte Raoul.

The *Comte* was carrying his gun on his shoulder and he smiled at Jean-Pierre when he saw him.

"Hello, what are you doing here?" he asked.

Then he looked over the boy's head at Larisa and she saw the gladness in his eyes.

"We came to warn you," she said when she reached him.

"To *warn me?*" he asked.

"There is a gun trap in the field," she said breathlessly. "Bernard set it after you had left. I was afraid you might go and look at it because there is a lamb in it."

"How do you know this?" Comte Raoul asked quietly.

"Monsieur le Comte said we were not to go out this morning because there would be gun traps set for the fox," Larisa answered, "so we went up to the roof."

"And you saw Bernard set it after I had passed through the field?"

Larisa nodded.

The Comte was still for a moment and then he said,

"I would of course have gone to see why the lamb was bleating. Once again, Larisa, I am in your debt."

Quite suddenly the full implication of what Monsieur le Comte had planned swept over her so that she felt as if the Comte's face swam before her as she said in a whisper.

"I am frightened!"

"It will be all right!" Comte Raoul said. "I will speak to my father. I have a suspicion there was no fox and that this was just a ruse to get me out of the house."

"If we had not gone on the roof," Larisa said in a low voice, "you might have been killed!"

There was so much emotion in her voice that the Comte put out his hand and took hers.

For a moment he did not speak then almost beneath his breath he said,

"We cannot live like this! It is impossible!"

Then as he saw the anxiety and the pallor on Larisa's face he added,

"It is all right at the moment. I am safe and we will walk back to the house together."

Larisa took Jean-Pierre by the hand.

"Come along, Jean-Pierre," she said. "We are going home with your father."

Jean-Pierre pulled at the lead because Max was nosing around the brushwood lying on the ground.

"Hold on to Max tightly, Jean-Pierre," Larisa said. "Would you like me to take him?"

"No, I will hold Max," Jean-Pierre replied.

He tugged at the dog again almost roughly as they all three set off along the path that led back to the garden.

"What are you going to say to Monsieur le Comte?" Larisa asked when they had walked a little way.

"It is hard to know how to begin," Comte Raoul replied with a sigh. "Even now I cannot believe it is true, that he really hates me to such an extent that he would do anything to be rid of me."

"And Bernard is involved in it too," Larisa said.

It somehow seemed worse that Monsieur le Comte with his dignity, his grandeur and his unmistakable authority should use as an accomplice a servant in an attempt to murder his own son.

It made the plot even more sinister than it would otherwise have been.

It was, Bernard who had poisoned the wine, Bernard who had set the gun trap.

Larisa could not help wondering what Monsieur le Comte would pay the man for his co-operation.

It was obvious that if they were successful and Comte Raoul died, Bernard would be able to blackmail Monsieur le Comte for the rest of his life.

Would he then have to murder his servant who had such a hold over him?

The whole thing was a kind of nightmare from which she longed to wake up to find it had no substance in fact.

But it was true, she thought.

True that if Comte Raoul had drunk the wine last night he would not now be walking beside her, and true too that the gun trap had been set in place after he had left for the woods and he had not been warned of its existence.

They were getting nearer to the trap and now Larisa could hear the lamb bleating.

She knew that Comte Raoul heard it too and he turned his head in its direction to note where the trap had been situated.

She saw the sudden pain in his eyes and his lips tightened.

'This hurts him,' she thought, 'to think that his father should wish to destroy him. However bad a parent he may be, Raoul is still his son and their blood is the same.'

She had the feeling that Comte Raoul, must have been proud of his father when he was a little boy just as he had been proud of Valmont.

It was from 'belonging' that one achieved a feeling of security and trust, and for it to turn to something like this would hurt any man.

Perhaps especially one as perceptive as Comte Raoul.

That was the strange thing about him, Larisa thought. Although he had a reputation that shocked and horrified so many people, he was the most perceptive person she had ever met.

She fancied too, although she was certain most people would deny it, that he was extremely sensitive.

The garden door was just ahead of them, and then at the side of the path a small rabbit, which must have been crouching down in the thick grass hoping to be unobserved, sprang up and started to streak across the field.

Max let out a yelp and wrenched the lead from Jean-Pierre's hand to go after it.

"Stop, Max! *Stop!*" Jean-Pierre cried.

Then he was running after his dog.

It all happened so quickly that Larisa hardly had time to realise it before Jean-Pierre was tearing across the field in pursuit of Max who was yelping after the rabbit.

She screamed "The trap! *The trap!*" and moved forward.

As if he too suddenly realised what was happening, Comte Raoul, who had been moving on ahead, turned back and started to run.

He was hampered by the gun and by the fact that Jean-Pierre had several yards start on them both.

Larisa was running and at the same time she was holding her breath.

Suddenly there was a violent explosion.

It rang out deafeningly, ringing in her ears, and she saw Jean-Pierre fall to the ground.

She tried to reach him but Comte Raoul was there before her.

He was bent over the little boy then as she came nearer he stood up and turned towards her.

"Do not look!" he said – and the words were a command. "Go to the *Château* and get help."

For a moment she could not obey him, but he put his hand on her shoulder and turned her round and she knew it was because he did not wish her to see Jean-Pierre.

"Do as I say!" he said, "and get two of the menservants to come here immediately!"

She could not speak and it was hard to get her breath but she did as he commanded.

She started to run frantically towards the gate in the wall.

She pulled it open and still running reached the door of the *Château* with her breath coming sobbingly from between her lips.

She moved into the cool passage, not quite certain which direction to take. Then, coming towards her, she saw the dark, sinister face of Bernard.

For a moment she hardly recognised him in her agitation.

"What's happened, *M'mselle?*" he asked.

"Go at once and take someone with you," she said. "The gun trap . . ."

As she spoke she thought there was a sudden gleam in the man's dark eyes.

"Is someone hurt?" he asked.

"*Le petit Monsieur!*" she replied, "Jean-Pierre!"

It seemed to her that Bernard's face was transformed into a mask of horror.

"Monsieur Jean-Pierre?" he repeated and his voice was gratingly harsh.

"Find someone and go to Comte Raoul immediately!" Larisa said again.

She leant back against the wall feeling as if she was being suffocated by a compression in her breast and the effort of getting her breath.

Bernard turned on his heel and walked down the passage in the direction in which he had come.

Larisa found it impossible to move and could only lean against the wall fighting a sudden faintness, trying to compose herself, trying to realise what had happened.

She knew that Jean-Pierre was dead. He had been killed by the gun trap that had been set for his father.

Two footmen came running down the passage towards her.

When they saw her, they stopped.

"We have been told there has been an accident, *M'mselle*. Where is it? Where are we to go?"

"In the field outside the garden," Larisa managed to gasp. "And hurry. *Monsieur* Raoul is there. He will tell you what to do."

The footmen disappeared through the open door into the garden and slowly, as if she were a very old woman hardly able to walk, Larisa found her way to the staircase.

Holding onto the bannisters she pulled herself up the stairs until she reached the first floor and then up again.

She wanted to find Nurse.

She knew she had to tell her what had happened and that she must prepare her for the body that the footmen and Comte Raoul would bring back to the house.

Nurse was in the schoolroom as Larisa had expected.

She was sitting at the table darning one of Jean-Pierre's little white socks.

She looked up as Larisa entered and saw her face and rose to her feet.

"What has happened?" she asked.

"He is . . . *dead!*" Larisa gasped and seeing the expression in the old woman's eyes added hastily,

"No – not Comte Raoul . . . Jean-Pierre!"

"Jean-Pierre?" Nurse exclaimed incredulously.

"He ran into the gun trap Bernard had set for Comte Raoul. I have not seen him . . . but I know he is . . . dead!"

The words came gasping from between her lips and she sat down in a chair at the table and put her head in her hands.

"I should not have taken him into the field after Monsieur le Comte told me not to," she said in a whisper, "but I had to save Comte Raoul."

She felt Nurse's hand on her shoulder.

Then as she buried her face, still fighting against faintness, still trying to think coherently, she felt Nurse put a glass into her hand.

"Drink this, *M'mselle*" she said quietly, "and I will make you a cup of tea."

Larisa lifted her head and now tears were streaming down her face.

"It is so horrible! So brutal! So unnecessary!"

Nurse did not answer, but surprisingly she was not crying as she busied herself with boiling the kettle on the fire that was burning in the grate even though it was such a warm day.

"Monsieur le Comte meant to . . . kill Comte Raoul," Larisa said almost as though she spoke to herself.

"I felt sure he would try again after you had saved him last night," Nurse said. "He is no longer sane! We have to face that fact, *M'mselle*. He is no longer sane!"

"How can we ever . . . tell him," Larisa asked, "that Jean-Pierre is . . . *dead?*"

"Who knows it now?" Nurse enquired.

"I met Bernard in the passage," Larisa answered. "He was expecting to hear that his trap had lured Comte Raoul."

"You told him that Jean-Pierre was dead?"

"I told him to go and help Comte Raoul," Larisa answered, "and he sent two footmen. When I told them where to go I came upstairs to you."

"Then Bernard will have told Monsieur le Comte what has happened," Nurse said. "There is no need for you to break the news to him."

"How will he bear it?" Larisa asked. "He loved the child."

"But he hated his son," Nurse answered, and her voice was hard.

"It was my fault," Larisa said. "If I had not taken him with me, he would still be alive. Monsieur le Comte said that we were to stay in the *Château*."

"It was an accident?" Nurse asked.

"Max ran after a rabbit," Larisa explained, "and Jean-Pierre went after the dog. I do not think Max was hurt, but Jean-Pierre must have run straight into the trap."

She gave a little sob. It was impossible to speak the last word.

Even now she could hardly realise it had happened.

One moment Jean-Pierre had been holding her hand and they had been walking beside Comte Raoul.

The next minute they had all been running across the field desperately trying to catch the child, to save him from the diabolical instrument of death set there by Bernard.

'How could Monsieur le Comte and his servant have concocted anything so cruel or so horrible?' Larisa asked herself.

Yet if the Comte had died it would have been difficult to prove it had been anything but an accident.

She could see it all so clearly, the way Monsieur le Comte had sent Comte Raoul to look for the fox, how he had warned her and Jean-Pierre not to go into the garden.

Who would ever be able to say he had not warned his son that there would be gun traps in the field, of which he must be careful?

No-one would doubt Monsieur le Comte's word and if he had succeeded it would have been the body of Comte Raoul they were bringing back to the house and Jean-Pierre would be as his grandfather had intended, the heir to Valmont.

If it had not been so tragic, Larisa thought, it would seem almost poetic justice that Monsieur le Comte should have destroyed the person he loved best, the person for whom he was prepared to commit the crime of murder.

Even knowing what she did about Jean-Pierre, that he was not normal and was beginning to show, although she hardly dare express it to herself, the unpleasant tendencies of the mentally disturbed, she would not wish the child dead.

In many ways she had loved the little boy.

It was only when she thought of what lay ahead for him in the future that she had felt apprehensive and afraid. Nurse set a cup of hot, strong tea down in front of Larisa and she drank it because she knew it would please the old woman.

It also took away, as it was intended to do, the feeling of faintness. After she had drunk it, Larisa wiped away her tears.

She had to be sensible about this.

She had to think not of herself but of Comte Raoul.

What, she wondered, would he say to his father?

Would he now face him with the fact that he had twice tried to murder him and only succeeded in killing his grandson?

She wanted so much to help him and yet she felt helpless.

"What do you think is happening?" she asked Nurse in a low voice.

"That is what I am going to find out," Nurse answered. "Stay here, *M'mselle*. There is nothing you can do. I'll do everything that needs to be done."

"I feel I should go with you," Larisa said.

Nurse shook her head.

"No," she said, "Monsieur Raoul would not wish it – I feel sure of that! Stay where you are!"

She went from the nursery and shut the door behind her.

As she had spoken so positively Larisa stayed sitting at the table supporting her aching head in her hands.

She knew Nurse was right when she said that Comte Raoul would not wish her to see anything that was unpleasant – not even poor little Jean-Pierre when he was dead.

He would want to protect her from all that was ugly and beastly, and besides at a moment like this she was not one of the family.

She was an outsider and it was only someone like Nurse, who had been with the Valmonts all her life, who could be a part of their suffering.

It was hard to wait and remain inactive only to wonder desperately what was happening.

They would bring Jean-Pierre back to the house.

Would they bring him up to his own bedroom?

She wished Nurse had not left her alone and she wondered if she should find Madame Savigny and tell her what had happened.

She shrank from speaking to anyone.

There would be too many questions she would have to answer, too many things she would have to explain.

Yet she could not sit still and rose from the table to walk about the room.

It was very warm because the fire was lit and she opened the windows as wide as they would go.

The schoolroom looked over the gardens on the South-East of the *Château*.

It looked very quiet, green, and empty.

It was difficult to think that so much drama and tragedy was taking place on the other side of the *Château*.

'They must have brought Jean-Pierre back by now,' Larisa thought.

What was happening? Why did no-one come to tell her?

She began to feel she could bear the suspense no longer.

She knew she was afraid to confront Comte Raoul in case he should blame her for what had occurred.

Why had she not held more tightly on to Jean-Pierre?

How could she have let him drag his little hand from hers?

She had never for one moment anticipated that he might release himself, and she knew he would not have done so had not the rabbit jumped up in front of Max.

It was such a natural, ordinary thing to happen!

Something that might occur a dozen times without there being anything unusual or tragic about it, but that it should have resulted in Jean-Pierre's death was something too horrible to contemplate.

'I cannot bear it! *I cannot bear it!*' Larisa said to herself.

She spoke aloud and moved towards the door.

She had to go downstairs to find out if by any miracle Jean-Pierre was still alive.

But even as she reached the door it opened and Nurse stood there.

"Where is he? Where have they put him?" Larisa asked. "Is he really . . . dead?"

"Jean-Pierre is dead," Nurse answered in a low voice, "and Monsieur le Comte has shot himself."

CHAPTER EIGHT

Nurse came into the schoolroom and Larisa looked up expectantly.

She had spent the whole morning, it seemed to her, waiting and yet the message she had hoped for had not come.

Now she held her breath.

"*Madame* would like to speak to you."

That was not what Larisa had wanted to hear.

At the same time it was better than sitting helplessly, longing to see Comte Raoul but knowing that it was very unlikely he would send for her.

She had learnt from Nurse what had happened yesterday afternoon.

The two bodies, Monsieur le Comte's and Jean-Pierre's, had been laid out by the women on the Estate. They were then taken to the Chapel where they would remain until the funeral.

Nurse told Larisa how before this Comte Raoul had sent for the local doctor and informed him there had been a shooting accident, which had killed both Jean-Pierre and Monsieur le Comte.

The doctor had signed the death certificates.

It then only remained for Comte Raoul to start making preparations for the huge family funeral which would be expected on the death of Monsieur le Comte.

Nurse had relayed to Larisa what was happening below and while she listened she found it impossible to restrain her tears. After some hours Nurse persuaded her to go to bed.

It was the shock of Jean-Pierre's death that had unnerved her, coming on top of the shock she had experienced the day before when she had thought she would not be in time to save Comte Raoul from the death that his father had prepared for him.

She was also physically tired from the ride to Paris and stiff because she had not ridden for some time.

There had been so much to do before she left home that she had not been able to ride every day as she had been accustomed to do before her father had died.

Everything combined to make her feel helpless and miserable.

She could not help blaming herself for Jean-Pierre's death and at the back of her mind was always the fear that Comte Raoul would blame her too.

All her thoughts were of him.

"How is he, Nurse?" she asked as soon as she awoke in the morning.

"Monsieur Raoul has been up since very early," Nurse answered. "He looks pale, as if he has not slept, but he is taking control of everything. There is a lot to be arranged."

"And Bernard? What has happened to Bernard?" Larisa enquired.

"He has disappeared!" Nurse replied. "It must have been the manner in which he told Monsieur le Comte that Jean-Pierre was dead that made him take his life. One of the footmen heard Bernard screaming out the news in a hysterical manner."

Nurse paused before she continued,

"I think he must have been terrified, knowing how fond Monsieur le Comte was of the little boy."

Larisa shivered.

"He has gone!" Nurse said, "and a good thing too! Otherwise Monsieur Raoul would have had to dismiss him!"

"Or bring him to justice?" Larisa suggested.

Nurse looked at her.

"Monsieur Raoul has made it very clear that what happened was a shooting accident," she said. "Monsieur le Comte was handling his gun when it exploded!"

It seemed an implausible story, Larisa thought. At the same time she knew that Comte Raoul would persuade his relatives that was what had occurred.

No questions would be asked.

She wondered as she went down the stairs and along the corridor to Madame Savigny's sitting room, whether the old lady would know the truth.

The room was in half-darkness owing to the fact that the blinds were drawn. Madame Savigny wearing black, was seated in her usual chair.

She looked up when Larisa entered and smiled.

"I have asked to see you, my dear," she said, "because Nurse tells me you are unhappy."

"What else could I be, *Madame*?" Larisa enquired as she moved forward.

She sat down in a low chair at Madame Savigny's side, who put out one of her blue-veined hands to touch Larisa's.

"It was God's will," she said quietly. "And perhaps it is for the best."

Larisa was sure that she was speaking of Jean-Pierre but for the moment she could not find words in which to ask the question which hovered on her lips.

"I think we both know," Madame Savigny went on, "that Jean-Pierre had not the capacity for learning what was expected of him."

Larisa looked at her wide-eyed.

"I did not dare to . . . say so."

"I knew that," Madame Savigny said, "and had you done so my brother would have dismissed you instantly!"

Larisa did not speak and after a moment Madame Savigny continued,

"But it would have had to be faced sooner or later, and so as I say perhaps God in His mercy knows what is best for us all."

"I hope so," Larisa murmured humbly.

"There are many things Raoul can do now to improve the property," Madame Savigny said. "I know how it has irked him that my brother would not tolerate any improvements or innovations. Raoul is young and enthusiastic, he will make Valmont what it was in our father's day, an example to all our neighbours."

She spoke with such pleasure that Larisa felt her spirits lifting a little.

"What is more," Madame Savigny said, "Raoul can now marry someone of his own choice and still help the estate."

Larisa felt as if she was turned to stone.

"You mean . . . ?" she began hesitatingly.

"I mean," Madame Savigny went on briskly, "that Raoul can find a bride amongst the noble families of Paris who will also have a large dowry."

She gave a little laugh.

"To be the mere heir to a big estate is a very different thing from already owning it. There is not a family in France who would not be proud to see their daughter married to Le Comte de Valmont."

It was impossible for Larisa to speak, and yet because she knew Madame Savigny was waiting for her response, she made a little strangled sound with her lips.

"Already," Madame Savigny said, "I have been compiling a list of the eligible young women whose parents would, I know, welcome Raoul with open arms. There are quite a number of them."

"Perhaps," Larisa said tentatively, "he might already be fond of someone... perhaps someone he knows, in Paris."

Madame Savigny shrugged her shoulders.

"I dare say there are a number of women with whom he has fancied himself enamoured," she said lightly, "but to a Frenchman, a *'chère amie'* is one thing, a wife another!"

"You ... mean," Larisa said in a very low voice, "that however fond Monsieur Raoul was of someone, if she was not ... eligible either in position or financially he would not marry her?"

"Of course not!" Madame Savigny said positively. "I suppose the English do not understand, but a Frenchman never marries his mistress, and all marriages amongst the *ancien régime* are *mariages de convenance.*"

There was a long silence before Larisa said,

"I was thinking, *Madame*, that I should return home. I can be of no further use now that Jean-Pierre is dead, and the funeral, which Nurse tells me will take place the day after tomorrow, is of course very much a family affair."

"I am sure, my dear, that you are right," Madame Savigny said. "The *Château* will be filled with relatives. Quite a number of them will be arriving this afternoon."

"Yes, of course," Larisa said.

She rose to her feet and then she said hesitatingly,

"I wonder Madame . . . if you could arrange for me to have the wages to which I am entitled for the time I have been here. I do not think otherwise I shall have . . . enough money for my return ticket."

"But of course," Madame Savigny answered. "I can understand you do not wish to worry my nephew at such a time. I will speak to his secretary. He will, I know, bring the money to your room where I expect you will be packing."

"I will," Larisa agreed. "And may I say goodbye, *Madame*, and thank you very much for your kindness to me?"

"I shall miss you, my dear," Madame Savigny said. "But I have a feeling now that my brother is dead that my life in the future will be very different from what it has been in the past. I feel sure my nephew, Raoul will look after me and I shall no longer feel trapped."

"I am sure he will," Larisa answered.

She curtsied and left the room, knowing that she was no longer of any particular interest to Madame Savigny who was obviously concerned only in what the future held for herself.

Larisa went up to her bedroom, ordered her trunks to be brought to her and started to pack.

Two housemaids helped her, and when her trunks were nearly full she sent one of them down to ask if she could have a carriage to take her to Paris.

The answer came back that the carriage would be ready in a quarter of an hour's time at a side-door.

When she received the message, Larisa could not help feeling that the staff had assessed her worth very accurately.

She was not of the 'quality', and therefore a side-door was the right place from which she should take her departure.

Nurse came into the room when she was already dressed in the travelling gown that had belonged to her mother, the little bonnet that matched it tied under her chin with blue ribbons.

"Do you wish to say goodbye to Monsieur Raoul?" Nurse asked,

"No," Larisa replied, "and promise me that you will not tell him I have gone unless he asks for me."

"You don't wish him to know?" Nurse asked in surprise.

Larisa hesitated for a moment and then she told the old woman the truth.

"I do not wish him to feel under any obligation because I rode to Paris to save him," she said. "He now has everything he wants in life, and I can be of no further . . . assistance to him."

There was a note in her voice that made Nurse look at her sharply. Then as if she felt it was none of her business, she obviously prevented herself from saying anything.

"Perhaps you are right, *M'mselle,*" she said after a moment.

"I know I am," Larisa answered, "so please do not mention my departure to anyone. I am sure there will be a train leaving for Calais sometime this evening, and if I am too late to catch a boat, I can stay the night in a *pension.*"

"You have enough money?" Nurse asked.

"Yes, thank you," Larisa replied. "Madame Savigny arranged for me to receive my wages for the weeks I have been here."

"Then God bless you," Nurse said. "When you get home, *M'mselle*, do not worry yourself over what has happened."

"I will try not to," Larisa answered, knowing as she spoke that it would be impossible not to remember, not to think, not to feel.

But what was the point of saying so?

She bent down and kissed the old woman's cheek.

"Thank you," she said softly. "I shall always remember you – as I shall remember Valmont."

Holding her head high she went down the stairs to the side-door where the carriage was waiting.

It was only as the carriage moved up the drive that she looked back. The *Château* with the sun on it was looking incredibly beautiful and the tears came into her eyes.

She had never known that a house could be so perfect, and yet it was not to the house she was saying goodbye but to its owner. With an almost superhuman effort she forced herself not to cry but think only of what lay ahead.

Once back in England she would have to find another position so that she could help Nicky.

It was unlikely there would be any such well-paid ones, and she thought apprehensively of the domestic bureaux she would have to write to or visit in the hope of finding a situation.

Would she ever be so lucky again? And yet, she asked herself, had she been lucky?

She had fallen in love irrevocably with a man who could never marry her and had broken her heart in consequence.

It was inevitable, she thought, that this should happen.

How could she possibly resist anyone as attractive as Comte Raoul?

How could she be expected to withstand his charm, to remain indifferent to the things he had said to her?

Words that had made her heart turn over in her breast and like his kiss had brought her an ecstasy which was not of this world.

She knew as she drove along the road to Paris that she was leaving behind at Valmont everything that mattered to her in life and ever would matter.

There was no point in deceiving herself.

This was the most tremendous, the most overwhelming, the most wonderful thing that had ever happened, and she knew if she was honest with herself, no other man could ever be the same for her.

Comte Raoul's love and the flame he had evoked within her had swept her up to the stars.

They had been part of the moonlight, part of Heaven itself, and anything else would in comparison be banal, mundane, and commonplace.

'I will love him all my life!' Larisa told herself and knew that merely to think of him was to feel herself quiver and her lips yearn for the touch of his.

She thought of the moment that he had kissed her hand, the first night when they had sat beneath the statue of Aphrodite and he told her that, what they felt for each other was 'different'.

Perhaps there were moments when they had been together that he would remember.

Perhaps he would think of her as he chose the wife who would bring new prosperity to Valmont and doubtless buy him the vineyard in the champagne district that he wanted so desperately.

Larisa did not feel bitter that she could do none of these things for him.

Comte Raoul had loved her in his own way, she was sure of it, but the call of duty and the obligation to Valmont and his family were in his blood.

Her mother had warned her, and she had not understood.

Now she had learnt that for a Frenchman duty came before all else – only she had learnt it at the expense of her heart.

The carriage reached the suburbs of Paris and she remembered how she had ridden through them frantically trying to find her way to the *Champs-Élysées*.

She wondered if Comte Raoul's friends whom he had entertained at the *Folies Bergères* or the alluring Odette had learnt that he was now Monsieur le Comte, the owner of Valmont.

If they did not know already, they would doubtless read of it in the newspapers.

Larisa wondered if they would be afraid of losing him now that he had a more important, responsible position.

But Madame Savigny had made it very clear that the two worlds never encroached on each other.

Between the *Beau Monde* and the *demi-monde* there was a great barrier, a gulf that could never be bridged except by a man who could pass from one to the other with the greatest of ease.

Once again Larisa felt very ignorant and unsophisticated. She had supposed that one of those beautiful women she had seen with Comte Raoul in the *Folies Bergères* was his mistress.

Perhaps the lady in red who had put her hand on his arm and pouted her lips at him alluringly because he had risen to leave her.

Odette must also be of the *demi-monde* Larisa thought.

She was certainly not the wife of His Serene Highness, whoever he might be, and yet he appeared to have a proprietory interest in her. If so, why did she look at Comte Raoul with love in her eyes?

It was all too complicated and difficult to understand.

But it seemed to Larisa as if the faces of the women were engraved in her mind, so that every time she thought of them, they appeared more fascinating, more lovely and she herself sank further into insignificance.

The carriage arrived at the *Gare du Nord*.

The journey had taken a little under an hour.

The footman got down to give her trunks to a porter. Larisa thanked the man and tipped him, although he did not seem to expect it, then went to the booking office.

The clerk told her there would be a train in three quarters of an hour. It was not the express, which had left earlier, and would therefore not reach Calais until late. Larisa purchased a second-class ticket and calculated she would have enough money to stay the night in Calais so long as she found a reasonable hotel or *pension*.

There was still the boat to be paid for and her railway fare to London, but she was certain she could manage it.

At the same time, she told herself, she must not be unnecessarily extravagant, or spend very much money on food.

She put her ticket into her bag and following the porter who had her luggage piled on a truck, went onto the platform.

The train was not yet in and she sat down rather gingerly on the edge of the truck hoping it would not spoil her gown.

There was the noise of hissing steam, of whistles being blown and the chattering of voices on other platforms.

With every incoming train the cry of, *'Porteur! Porteur!'* was echoed and re-echoed calling the blue-bloused porters with their black berets on their dark heads.

At any other time, Larisa would have been interested in the French children, the newspaper sellers and the passengers.

Now she could only think of what she had left behind.

Time passed slowly but at last the porter came back to her side.

"The train arrives, *Madame.*"

It came steaming into the station belching clouds of smoke, and a crowd of passengers seemed to spring from nowhere shouting, jostling and pushing their way to the carriages.

"I'll find you a seat, *Madame*," the porter said, "and then I'll put your trunks in the van."

"*Merci bien!*"

He picked up Larisa's holdall and she turned to follow him, only to find a tall figure barring her path.

She looked up automatically and then was frozen where she stood.

It was Comte Raoul who faced her, looking she thought with a sinking of her heart, as angry as he had been the first time she had seen him.

He had the face of the devil!

"Where do you think you are going?" he demanded, and his voice seemed almost like a whiplash.

"A-away."

"That is obvious!" he retorted, "but why?"

"I have to . . . go," she replied. "I am no longer . . . wanted at . . . Valmont."

"Who said you were not wanted?"

"There was nothing more for me to do."

"*I* will decide that!"

With an effort she dropped her eyes from his furious face.

"I must go."

"Not until we have talked things over."

"There is nothing to talk about," she said quickly. "I have to leave. I *have* to."

"There will be other trains."

The *Comte* turned to the porter who came back at that moment to say,

"I've taken a seat for you, *Madame.*"

"Bring the baggage to the entrance," Comte Raoul said curtly. "*Madame* is not leaving on this train."

The porter recognised the tone of command, collected Larisa's holdall from where he had left it and, pulling his truck, followed them down the platform.

Larisa wanted to protest, to insist that she took the train as she had planned, but somehow it was impossible to find the words.

She walked beside Comte Raoul feeling like a child who had played truant and been caught out.

At the same time, she told herself, she knew what he was going to suggest, and it was something that she must not even contemplate, let alone agree to.

'I must be firm,' she told herself.

She felt as if her whole being had melted because he was beside her and that she was weak with the same breathless wonder which always crept over her whenever they were together.

Outside the station she saw his phaeton and knew by the sight of the sweating horses the rate at which he must have travelled.

The groom stepped down to hand Comte Raoul the reins.

He took his place in the driving seat and meekly Larisa sat down beside him.

"Bring the baggage to the house, Jacques," Comte Raoul said and drove off.

As they moved through the traffic Larisa knew where they were going, and it only added to her conviction within herself as to what the *Comte* intended to say to her.

He had told her before that she could not go to his house in Paris because she was of the *Beau Monde,* and it was a bachelor establishment.

Now he had changed his mind, and because he was opening his door to her, she knew into which category she now fitted.

She thought of her mother, but somehow her family in England seemed very far away.

There was only the Comte. She had not seen her last of him as she had thought, but he was here beside her.

She was vividly conscious of the vibrations emanating from him.

She stole a glance at him from under her eyelashes and saw that he was still looking angry.

Yet with his tall hat on one side of his dark head, his high collar and broad shoulders, he looked irresistibly attractive so that her heartbeat suffocatingly because she was close to him.

'*I love him!*' she thought desperately, 'but I have to be strong. I have to say no!'

They drove through the *Place de la Concorde* and up the *Champs-Élysées*. The chestnuts were in bloom and their pink and white blossoms looked like Christmas candles against their dark leaves.

Children's merry-go-rounds and the balloon sellers were vivid patches of colour against the perambulating crowds.

The horses moved a little higher up the avenue and came to a stop outside the *Comte's* house.

A groom ran forward to go to the horses' heads and the *Comte* stepped down.

He put out his hand to Larisa to help her alight and she felt herself thrill at his touch, even though she told herself severely it was something she should not do.

They entered the hall where she had stood talking with his manservant the night she had been trying to find where he might be.

The *Comte* handed his hat and gloves to the doorman, then walked towards a door, which was opened for him, and made a gesture for Larisa to precede him into a room.

It was a large and very lovely salon decorated in the same exquisite taste that characterised Valmont.

There were windows opening out onto a small marble courtyard, which was brilliant with flowers.

But Larisa had eyes only for the *Comte* as she turned round to face him.

The door shut behind them and they were alone.

"I want an explanation!" he said before she could speak.

"I am doing what is right for me and best for. . . you," Larisa replied.

She knew as she spoke that it was right.

She loved him with her whole heart, her body and her soul, and yet she knew that whatever he might say to her she could not stay with him as his mistress.

It would defame and spoil their love.

It would ruin the beauty and the wonder that had enveloped them like a halo when they had talked together under the statue of Aphrodite and when he had kissed her in the drive at Valmont.

It had been so perfect, so much a part of her belief in God that just to be with him, she could not spoil those moments of wonder.

"I must be very dull-witted," the *Comte* said, "but I have not the least idea what you are talking about."

Larisa twisted her fingers together.

She had drawn off her gloves without thinking, and now they dropped to the floor but the Comte made no effort to pick them up.

"You have to marry," she said in a low voice. "You can now choose your own bride, but as you well know she had to be someone of whom your family will approve and who will bring you a big dowry. Valmont cannot survive without it!"

"Who has told you this?" Comte Raoul asked.

"I have known it ever since we talked together in the garden," Larisa replied, "and today your Aunt told me that was what you were expected to do."

"You did not think it wise to consult me before you rushed out of the house without even saying goodbye?"

"I could not bear to do that," Larisa whispered.

He walked away from her to stand a moment looking out into the garden.

"There are so many explanations I have to make to you," he said, "but I believed that you would understand that I had first to arrange my father's funeral and Jean-Pierre's."

"I did understand," Larisa said, "but I thought too you might be . . . angry with me for not looking after Jean-Pierre better. It was my fault that I did not hold on to him more firmly."

"It was no-one's fault," the *Comte* said positively. "Besides surely you and I can speak frankly to each other, Larisa. We both know there could be no future for Jean-Pierre."

"You . . . knew?" she asked in a low voice.

"One of the many governesses my father dismissed because they told him the truth," Comte Raoul replied, "came to see me before she left Paris."

"And you did nothing about it?"

"What could I do?" he asked. "You know as well as I do that my father was convinced the child was clever. He would not have heeded a whole panel of doctors who told him different, let alone anything I could say."

"I am sorry," Larisa said, "it must have been very . . . painful for you that you should have a son like that."

There was a moment's silence and then Comte Raoul said quietly,

"Jean-Pierre was not my son!"

He had his back to Larisa as he spoke and for a moment she thought she had not heard him aright.

Then he turned round.

"It was one of the things I was going to tell you when you were prepared to listen to me."

"B-but . . . how? I-I do not . . . understand?" Larisa stammered.

The *Comte* walked back across the room towards her.

"My father made me marry because the union would be an advantageous one for the estate," he said. "The girl who became my bride also had no choice in the matter, and on our wedding-night she informed me she hated me. She was in love with someone else and she was already bearing his child."

The *Comte* turned to walk restlessly across the room and stand once again looking at the courtyard.

"I never touched her!"

"And you did not tell your father this?" Larisa asked.

"Do you imagine he would have believed me?" the Comte enquired. "He had the grandson he wanted. That was all that concerned him."

Larisa put her hand up to her forehead.

"It is all so difficult to understand."

The Comte turned round.

"This is too much for you on top of what happened yesterday," he said. "I imagined you were resting. When I learnt you had left the *Château* I thought I should go mad!"

Their eyes met and for a moment it seemed as if neither of them could breathe and that explanations were unnecessary.

Then with an effort Larisa looked away and sat down in a chair.

Automatically, not realising what she was doing, she undid the ribbons of her bonnet and drew it from her head.

The *Comte* stood looking at the golden glow of her hair against the dark velvet chair in which she was sitting before he said quietly,

"You have still not told me why you thought it was right for you to go away?"

"I think I know what you are perhaps going to suggest to me," Larisa answered, "and it would spoil what we have felt for each other. I accept that you must marry the right person, but perhaps because I am English I could not . . . share you or take the only position in your life that is . . . open to me."

She spoke hesitatingly and he could hardly hear the words.

As she finished, she looked up at him and saw his eyes blazing at her. It made him seem more frightening than he had before.

"How dare you!" he exclaimed. "How dare you even imagine – let alone tell me – that I would ask you to

become my mistress! Did I not tell you that what I felt for you was different? Do you not know by now that I love you as I have never loved any woman before?"

His tone was so angry that Larisa felt herself tremble, and yet there was a strange flame of excitement moving within her.

"But . . . Frenchmen do not marry . . . for love!" she stammered.

For the first time he smiled, and it transformed his face.

"You think you know all the answers," he said, and now his voice was no longer angry but caressing. "Oh, my ridiculous, absurd, foolish little Aphrodite, do I have to spell it out to you in words of one syllable that this Frenchman is different?"

He bent down to pull her to her feet and into his arms.

"I am asking you to marry me, my darling!" he said very softly.

Larisa was quivering because she was so close to him, because the whole room seemed to be full of sunshine, gold and blinding. Then she said,

"But you have to marry for money!"

"Are you afraid of being poor with me?" he enquired.

"No, of course not!" Larisa said quickly.

"You would stay at Valmont without fantastic parties, beautiful dresses or fabulous jewels?"

"I only wanted those things so that you would admire me," Larisa answered, "and I cannot imagine anything nearer to Heaven than to be at Valmont with you!"

He bent his head and found her lips.

Just for a moment she put out her hands as though she would resist him, and then the room whirled around her and once again the ecstasy and the wonder she had known before when he kissed her in the drive at Valmont swept over her.

Now he was carrying her not into a starlit sky but towards the sun, and she was conscious only of trying to move closer and still closer to him so that they were one person.

Finally, he raised his head and looked down at her shining eyes, at her lips warm and trembling from his kiss.

"I love you!" he said, and his voice was hoarse. "I love you and nothing else is of any consequence except you!"

"You should not have come here after me," Larisa said. "There is so much for you to do at Valmont. Your family will be arriving."

"Do you think they matter beside the fact that I might have lost you?" the *Comte* asked. "Have you not realised yet, my precious, that I will never let you go?"

He saw the wonder in her eyes and then she hid her face against his shoulder.

"There is the vineyard," she murmured, "and all the new implements on the farm. Have you forgotten that?"

"I bought the vineyard!" he answered, "and you shall help me order the new implements next week."

She raised her head to look at him incredulously.

"I am a very rich man, my darling," he said. "Not that it matters beside the fact that you would have stayed with me even had I been poor."

"But . . . how?" Larisa enquired.

"My father saved and hoarded every penny, and the money has been accumulating. I could never understand why he said he was so hard-up, because I knew my grandfather had left a considerable fortune and it would have been difficult for it all to be dissipated so quickly. Now I find I can do everything I want to do. You shall have your dresses, my lovely one, and the jewels that go with them."

Larisa drew in her breath and then she said,

"Are you sure? Quite sure you should marry me? What will your family think and say? After all, to them I am . . . only a governess."

The *Comte* laughed and held her a little closer.

"I imagine your status, my beautiful little goddess, is about the same socially as that of a tout for champagne!"

Larisa looked up at him.

"I do not understand."

"How do you suppose," he asked, "I have existed all these years without one penny from my father and having no income of my own?"

"There was your wife's dowry," Larisa said hesitatingly.

"I sent it back!" he said. "That was another thing that infuriated my father, for when my wife died, I returned both the dowry and the land to her family. I would not wish to benefit from a marriage that had been an utter farce!"

He looked into Larisa's wide eyes and continued,

"But I still had to live! When I first came to Paris, I achieved a reputation for being wild, dashing and extravagant in a very short space of time."

He smiled.

"Because of such dubious notoriety I was approached by the famous champagne firm of Moet and Chandon."

"What did they ask you to do?"

"Merely to promote their champagne, especially their Dom Perignon, by drinking it," the Comte replied. "It sounds simple, does it not?"

"They paid for your parties?" Larisa asked.

"My parties, my horses, my house, my clothes – everything!" the *Comte* replied.

He gave a sigh.

"They were very kind. At the same time, I cannot tell you how sick I am of parties, of thinking up original forms of entertainment for the purpose of publicity, of drinking nothing but the delectably superlative Dom Perignon!"

"So that was why you wanted a case of your own wine?"

"It was just for myself," the *Comte* said, "and if you had not saved me, one glass would have caused my death!"

Larisa gave a little murmur and hid her face against him.

"But I am alive, my darling!" he said, "and so, as soon as the funeral is over and my family have returned to their homes, we will be married very quietly either at Valmont or else in England. The choice is yours."

"Do you mean that?" Larisa cried. "I would love above all things for Mama and the girls to see Valmont, and Nicky could give me away."

She gave a little exclamation.

"Nicky! You know I promised . . . that was why I was working . . ."

". . . to let him stay at Oxford," the Comte finished. "I think I might contrive to find enough money to ensure that my wife does not have to work!"

He paused and then with his lips very close to hers he said,

"Except for me, of course!"

"You know that I will do anything that you want me to do," Larisa whispered.

"That is a very big promise," he answered, "and I shall hold you to it!"

He tightened his arms until his lips were touching hers.

"It is going to take me a lifetime," he said very softly, "to explain to you how different what we feel for each other is, and how much you mean to me."

She thought he was going to kiss her, and her lips were soft and ready for his. Then he said,

"But I am still angry with you for not trusting me, for believing for one moment that I would hurt or damage what lay between us by treating you as one of the *demi-monde*."

"You brought me . . . here," Larisa said.

He gave a little laugh.

"So, you remembered that did you? Then let me set your mind at rest, by telling you that my maternal grandmother is at this moment in the house. She is staying here the night as she is too old to travel long distances and will come to Valmont tomorrow. You are very efficiently chaperoned, my love!"

"You think of everything!" Larisa said softly.

"As I always shall where you are concerned," he answered. "Only I warn you . . ."

He paused and lifted her chin up so that she should look at him.

". . . if you try to escape me again," he said, "I shall prove to you very forcibly that my nickname is justified. You are mine, Larisa, *mine* now and for always and I will never let you go!"

She felt herself quiver at the deep note of sincerity in his voice.

Then masterfully he swept her against him holding her so tightly that it was almost impossible to breathe and his mouth was on hers.

He kissed her violently, passionately, fiercely.

There was no gentleness in his lips, only the demanding insistence of a conqueror who has vanquished every enemy and glories in his triumph.

Larisa felt the fire burning within him engender the flame already mounting in her breasts.

She was no longer afraid.

She was his and she knew that he was hers.

They were one and he carried her towards the burning glory of the sun.

Printed in Great Britain
by Amazon